RELAX

CW01669076

MEDITA

FOR BASIC GUIDED RELAXATION

A Collection of Wonderful and Relaxing Stories Specially Created to Help you Sleep Peacefully and Heal

By

SLEEP LIKE A LOG

© Copyright 2021 by SLEEP LIKE A LOG - All rights reserved.

This document is geared towards providing exact and reliable information concerning the topic and issue covered. The publication is sold with the idea that the publisher is not required to render accounting, officially permitted, or otherwise, qualified services. If advice is necessary, legal or professional, a practiced individual in the profession should be ordered. From a Declaration of Principles which was accepted and approved equally by a Committee of the American Bar Association and a Committee of Publishers and Associations.

In no way is it legal to reproduce, duplicate, or transmit any part of this document in either electronic means or in printed format. Recording of this publication is strictly prohibited and any storage of this document is not allowed unless with written permission from the publisher. All rights reserved.

The information provided herein is stated to be truthful and consistent, in that any liability, in terms of inattention or otherwise, by any usage or abuse of any policies, processes, or Instructions: contained within is the solitary and utter responsibility of the recipient reader. Under no circumstances will any legal responsibility or blame be held against the publisher for any reparation, damages, or monetary loss due to the information herein, either directly or indirectly.

Respective authors own all copyrights not held by the publisher.

The information herein is offered for informational purposes solely and is universal as such. The presentation of the information is without a contract or any type of guarantee assurance.

The trademarks that are used are without any consent and the publication of the trademark is without permission or backing by the trademark owner. All trademarks and brands within this book are for clarifying purposes only and are owned by the owners themselves, not affiliated with this document.

Table of Contents

RELAXING BEDTIME MEDITATION STORIES FOR BASIC GUIDED RELAXATION.....1
Spring Shoots.....6
The Direction of the Sailboat.....14
Melting into the Flames of the Sun.....23
Breaking the Shell.....31
The Secret of Nature.....40
Floating alongside the Universe.....49
With a Great Friend.....58
A Beautiful Walk on the Sand.....67
An Oasis to Dream.....76
A Journey through the Beautiful Horizon.....84
A Magical Waterfall.....92
The Great Lake that Became my Purpose.....101
The Great Seat of Silence.....110
Dancing in a Sacred Place.....119
Happiness and Music.....129
Inner Strength.....139

The Great Rock, My Great Purpose.............147
The Butterfly, the Child, and the Context.......156
A Garden of Dreams...............................166
The Island of Enchantment........................175
A Visit to Heaven................................184
The Jungle of Dreams.............................193
A Delicious Break................................201
The Streets of Calm..............................210
A Walk along the Beach...........................219
Rest in the Snow.................................227

Spring Shoots

Greetings, friend, I welcome you to this comforting and serene space made especially for you. It is a pleasure to know that you have allowed yourself a moment of relaxation and harmony; also you have allowed me to accompany you on this path so that together we can achieve your freedom from worries and feel full peace because it is positive that you give yourself a break from your environment so that you transform your energies into new and positive ones.

(Medium pause)

I invite you to look for a quiet space where you can lie down and feel comfortable with your interior and exterior. If you got that place to your liking, we can do a breath that helps you release tension and relax you to start with meditation. Let's take a delicate bite of air and we will stretch our arms and back as much as we can, you hold your breath for a count of 5 and while you slowly expel the air, you can take the posture you had.

(Long pause)

Before starting the adventure that awaits you, it is important that just as your body is relaxed, your mind also enters a calm discarding every unnecessary thought and remembering those beautiful and positive moments that you lived: like when you did a good deed towards someone without No matter what it was like or also think about when you simply enjoyed some time alone with yourself watching a beautiful sunset, focus on those happy images that come to your mind. You are feeling how you are becoming lighter and more pleasant, if there was ever a concern or displeasure, they disappeared because now you are in connection with the harmony of your being.

(Medium pause)

You are in a space of harmony, you looked for a moment for yourself because you want peace in your interior and connection with the nature of your being. Today you are here to appreciate the simplicity and perfection of life, your spirit, and your environment, you are here to be the best version of yourself.

(Short pause)

You are the harmony in a person.

You are made to shine.

You are special just as you are.

Your spirit is pure.

You radiate joy.

You are love.

You are beautiful.

You are accepting and grateful.

You are perfect.

You love me.

You are the root of prosperity.

(Medium pause)

You breathe gently, recharging your body with good vibes and blocking all external noise from you. Empty your mind little by little. I want you to keep in mind that if at some point you feel that you are falling asleep during meditation, calm down, flow with it, you and I can continue at another time with this encounter. Now, you perceive how a cool breeze goes up your feet, caressing your legs and hips, gently sliding until it reaches your neck and spreads towards your arms and face.

(Short pause)

You experience playful and pure energy that has taken you to a beautiful place filled with thick and bright green grass. Just seeing it makes you want to run, lie down and play with it, so you start to walk and feel a loving breeze that embraces each part of your body with sweetness and strips you of your clothes, making you free of ties and memories. You feel alive and happy to exist, to be you because you are calm and in connection with the earth and its simplicity

(Medium pause)

Even though in that place there is only the grass and you, there is something about it that attracts you and vibrates with you. Then, you decide to kneel resting on your calves, you stretch your arm caressing their long tips, and then you introduce your hands completely in the grass, burying your fingers in the refreshing Earth. Great energy of confidence begins to run through your arms and leaves in its wake delicate buds of tender and fresh leaves. That precious energy is still within you, it is running through your body and it will spring up in those spaces that you still do not accept.

(Medium pause)

Something interesting has happened in the place, where before there was only grass, now there is a small and delicate plant in the middle of the place, its appearance makes you curious and exciting at the same time. You get close to where she is and you sit next to her just watching her without judging her, just seeing her simple beauty. What do you think when you see it? Are you excited, touched, do you like it, do you admire it? How about you tell her what it causes you when you see her. You can start by telling her that she is beautiful, delicate, light up the place, give her all your love that counts until your silence because she needs it.

(Medium pause)

Now you observe your body and discover that another outbreak has occurred in you, they are different species of flowers that are located on your knee, back, shoulder, arm, and abdomen. A tingle of emotions lodges in your belly and you just want to run, live in the moment, so you glide with excitement through the place, jumping and feeling free. You feel comfortable with who you are and how you are.

(Medium pause)

By the time you stop, you end up lying under the beautiful tree that grew because of your pretty words and your love. But you notice that something else that changed in it, there are also flowers of different species and colors that harmonize its branches, you find the great beauty that arises from it dazzling, and suddenly, you visualize yourself being her. Now there is no tree but you are. It has always been you, with a strong and molded trunk that supports you in your walk, fresh and harmonious leaves that complement you and make you what you are today, and the flowers, they symbolize your natural beauty and your beautiful personality.

(Medium pause)

You became a beautiful spring bud because you believed in yourself, you fell in love with every part of your body, you found peace in your mind and soul, and you understood that you are the very beauty of nature. Today you listened and allowed yourself to change, now open yourself to look beyond that tree and listen to the whispering of the wind. You can see in the beautiful garden that that place became thanks to your love and roots of healing and prosperity. You have already managed to find your way, now you feel like your body is becoming one only with that space and you are sinking into the comfortable place where you rest. We meet another opportunity, rest my friend.

The Direction of the Sailboat

Welcome, friend, it is good to have you here today in this space for healing and relaxation of your body, mind, and spirit. I congratulate you for deciding that it is time to trust a little more and let yourself be guided by a new adventure. Giving yourself a short break in the day to concentrate and reactivate your good vibes is an action of intelligence, I am proud of you for being aware that you want a positive and harmonious change in your life and you seek to make it come true.

(Medium pause)

To start our great adventure, join me looking for a comfortable corner, sofa, or bed where you can rest freely so that your emotions and energies flow harmoniously within you. See that your body is stretched and your head and neck find a pleasant posture during all this time. If you have already found the place, close your eyes and let yourself be carried away by my voice that will lead you to a sea of imagination and you will float on the sailboat of your emotions.

(Medium pause)

Now I invite you to close your eyes and let go of your body and mind so that they disconnect from reality and immerse yourself in a sea of imagination. It is time to leave behind any discomfort, burden, or unnecessary thoughts because they are only there to take away positive energy. You take a soft mouthful of air and you feel how a bright and pure light enters your body and is freeing the space within you, you release it relieved and serene because you feel clean and healthy inside. We breathe in again, gently and slowly, hold the air for a count of 5, and then slowly expel it.

(Medium pause)

Today you have decided to try something new and positive for your life, you are here to free yourself from weights that do not let you flow in harmony. For that reason, together we will sail towards the full peace of your being, you will let go of the helm and you will let yourself be carried away by the wind and the sails of relaxation. I will be by your side accompanying you to the destination that will make you shine and rejuvenate your spirit because you are a dreamer on the high seas, you are that lantern of light that has not yet realized all its splendor.

(Medium pause)

You are light and harmonious.

You are a clean spirit.

You are love.

You are made of peace.

You're Smart.

You are the calm of the ocean itself.

You are in control of your emotions and your being.

You flow with the wind.

You drop the direction of life.

You are grateful.

You are hope.

You shine who surrounds you.

You are positive.

You are immense and unique.

(Medium pause)

You are listening to the beating of your heart: so serene, to the slow heart beat rhythm of, the vibration of your chest, and the precious way in which it communicates with you. Keep in mind that if at any time you fall asleep, calmly continue with your rest, because that means that you managed to find what you were looking for: your dream. You keep breathing, you enjoy how the air inflates your lungs and cleanses them of all impurities, making them purer and fresher.

(Medium pause)

You lose yourself in the serenity of your surroundings and feel a sweet light that appears wherever you are. It is shining so brightly that you transport yourself to a new place. The temperature is warm and cool at the same time, it is a quite pleasant and peaceful space. You hear a gentle wave that surrounds you, you let yourself be carried away by the sound that reaches your ears, and now you can see the immense ocean where you are, the beautiful blue sky with its pure clarity, the simple and innocent clouds that declare harmony. , the impressive sun that revitalizes you and the playful wind that dances around you caressing your skin. Just by looking at that landscape you nourish yourself with good vibes, your mind clears and your spirit feels free.

(Medium pause)

You find yourself floating on the high seas with a large sailboat, he declares himself at this moment the captain of your way to peace and full rest. You feel the positive and kind energy in every part of your body, you perceive its breath, its heartbeat, its life itself and you respect it. You go to the bow of the large wooden guide where you are and you sit crossing your legs. The gentle rocking produced by the waves when colliding with the ship makes you connect your essence with each part of it. You get to his spirit and you synchronize with him, you understand him and you understand that he is indicating your path and the meaning of your life.
(Medium pause).

Now you get up and decide to travel the sailboat, you agreed to be guided by it and you enjoy the journey it offers you. You enthusiastically look out on the deck and discover that you are not alone, that countless marine animals accompany you on the journey. You see a couple of whales accompanied by their calf that swims peacefully near the sailboat, their bodies come out of the water and then submerge in a small jump exposing their respective tails, causing a movement of waves that move the ship in their swaying. A little further on you see a group of naughty dolphins that jump and play among the immensity of the blue sea. The turtles swim past the boat so lightly that their large shells seem so light to them, agile, and full of so much history.

(Medium pause)

Everything you are experiencing comforts you emotionally, it helps you see the beauty of life and its great diversity, you appreciate the beauty of nature and the teaching received. Teaching that now allows you to appreciate the value of freedom, of letting flow, of letting go of ties that prevent you from evolving towards the best of you.

(Medium pause)

Now you breathe with more freedom, calm, serenity, and peace of your environment that is in you. You let yourself be carried away by the smoothness of the marine movement because you already realize that there are moments where it is necessary to trust and let go. You immerse yourself in the immensity of your inner sea, letting it take you to the place where you rest. We have reached your destination, good friend, now you can rest.

Melting into the Flames of the Sun

Hello, good friend, I give you a pleasant welcome to the place that fills you with inner peace and mental well-being. It is a joy to know that you are giving yourself a moment of rest and a relationship just for yourself. For that reason, this time we will travel spaces outside your reality, entering the immense and brilliant imagination that vibrates with great force and harmony within you.

(Medium pause)

To fully transfer us to this new adventure, I invite you to look for a small and cozy space where you can rest and free your mind and body. When you've found that ideal spot, you can settle in by turning off the light, sitting or lying down, and closing your eyes. In this way, we can connect with divine energy. Stretch your arms and back to release tensions and leave your mind in a pleasant position to the place so that it can flow with the vibes.

(Medium pause)

Now is the time to move your environment away from you. Begin by emptying your mind of any thoughts, discomfort, tension, or noise that is distracting your peace of mind. Let's do a soft breath: inhaling slowly through the nose and holding it for one, two, three and expel it slowly, repeat taking air again, this time, enjoy how it goes through your inside along with your veins, you will feel clean and relieved, at the count to five, you release all that air that has cleansed your body.

(Medium pause)

This is your space of trust and improvement. You are here to find the bright light of your path, to understand who you are and where you are going. Today you will begin to let go of the blocks and walk the lines that your destiny has marked with euphoria for you so that you discover the new pure, capable, vivacious, and empowered person that you will become and understand how valuable you are.

(Short pause)

You are the positive change.

You are the energy of prosperity.

You are light.

You are fiery.

You are important.

You are love.

You are part of something great.

You are important to the world.

You are brave.

You are one with the Universe.

You enjoy the fullness.

You give brightness and harmonious energy to those around you.

You are a vibrant star.

(Medium pause)

You feel the movement that your chest makes when you inhale and exhale, you let yourself be carried away by the perfect movement with which your body communicates. You listen to the strong beat of your heart and blood travel through your veins. Remember that if at some point all your senses are falling asleep, I want you to follow them, we can always meet another time. Now, you begin to perceive your lighter body, without any weight, as rising by the positive energy that propels you off the planet, through the dense atmosphere of relaxation floating in the deep and luminous space.

(Medium pause)

You admire each star, galaxy, and wonder that belongs and makes the Universe come to life, you got there for some reason, you feel part of that immensity, and you found the beginning of your destiny. You experience a pleasant tingling sensation on the balls of your feet, knees, hips, hands, and shoulders: a change is taking place within you, cosmic signals let you know that something extraordinary awaits you.

(Medium pause)

You are in infinite space with the density of dark blue and with the beautiful wonders that are illuminated by a higher star, by the king of the Universe, and in charge of everything in that space. Its brightness is an abnormal potential that benefits every little or great thing that lives around or far from it. There is something of that light that calls you, shouts you to be part of that whole, and illuminates your spirit towards your well-being, and helps those who need you.

(Medium pause)

Around you, two shooting stars begin to dance with a warm splendor, they leave mesmerizing flashes in their wake that form dazzling spirals and circles, their brightness envelops you in a harmony of peace with your being. Now they lead you through space, through galaxies of vibrant colors, jumping over the large rocks of hot gases that run through your body, activating it towards the adrenaline of desire and empowerment, and avoiding, every latent star in the Universe.

(Long pause)

You start to feel a warm glow that grows stronger as you get closer. Your curiosity is becoming more present in you, you have the hunger to know where your destiny takes you, what awaits you at the end of the journey. Then, you find yourself face to face with what you expected so much, a giant fireball models fiery eruptions in front of you, you feel how the fire gently caresses your skin and enters your pores activating all your spirit with fiery and positive energy that It opens doors to a change, to a new cycle of your being.

(Medium pause)

You are just a breath away from being immersed in the wild flames of the sun. Your eyes look like two large stars completely bright by the reflection of the light of the great star, and then, you push yourself towards its center, crossing each of its dense and viscous layers of lava, a soft and fluffy mixture of fire envelops you, empowering each centimeter of your existence. Turning you into light, flame ... into a splendid star.

(Medium pause)

You are emerging as a fiery star from the depth of the sun, you have become the new you, full of energy, with a desire to make a positive change in the world; illuminating those around you, and even those who listen to you. You have freed yourself from your bondage and overcame every obstacle. Now you descend at high speed towards the planet, dazzle the last corners of the dark Universe and cross the atmosphere like a great meteorite and sink in the gravity of the world to your comforting place of sleep. Inside you, you are still the bright star that melted and filled with the revitalizing energy of the sun. We have already reached the end of the journey that marked your destiny, we are in the next one. Have a good rest, my bright and vibrant friend.

Breaking the Shell

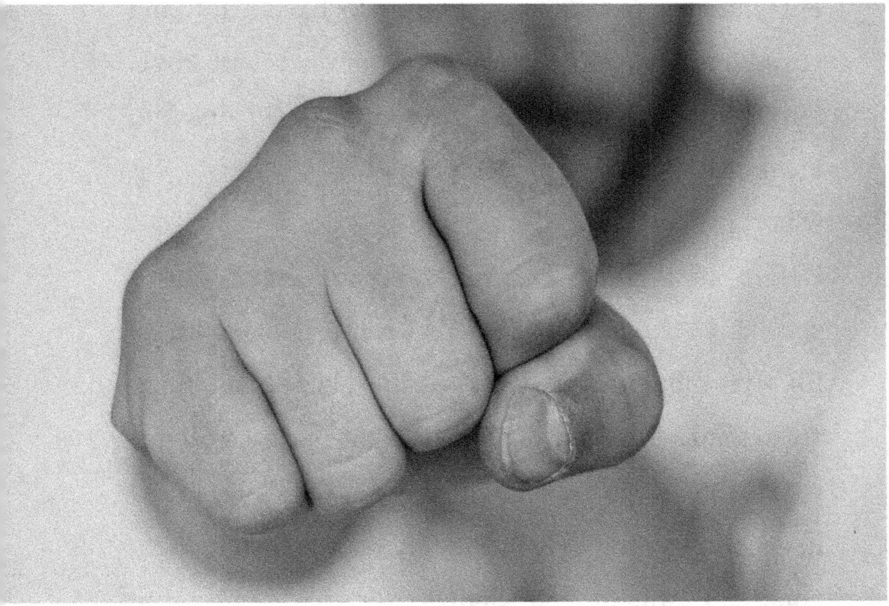

Hello, friend, welcome to this space of reconnection with your mind and spirit. I am glad that you have motivated yourself to undertake this rejuvenating adventure and that you also allow me to accompany you along the way. Keep in mind that you deserve everything you want, you deserve to have a full and stress-free rest. For that reason, today we will travel through the warmth of memories and we will sink into the dream of tranquility and peace.

(Short pause)

Before starting our session, I invite you to find a special place where you can feel comfortable and free for your mind to flow with positive energy and block all external discomfort related to unnecessary noise, worries, tensions, or thoughts. When you have found it, accompany me by gently lying on the site; keeping your back straight, and leaving your neck and head in a pleasant and serene position.

(Medium pause)

We have already found a comfortable and pleasant space for this adventure. Now, let's focus on your breathing, how slow or fast it is and we will stay there feeling its journey inside your body. Meanwhile, your mind is clearing those heavy vibes, managing to calm and rejuvenate them. Keep breathing, and this time, she gives you the freedom to guide her. Slowly take a mouthful of air and hold it for a count of five, at the end, expel it slowly through your mouth and repeat.

(Medium pause)

Continue with that calm breathing and little by little let it flow at its own pace again. It is time for you and me to focus on you, on what you are looking for and want to achieve. Today you are here to give yourself a break that helps you make a prosperous change in your life and allows you to be fully grateful to yourself and to the world, to be patient with the small steps that will guide you with determination on your path.

(Short pause)

You are brilliant.

You are determined.

You are full of calm.

You are optimistic.

You are important.

You are love.

You have the virtue of patience.

You are motivated.

You motivate people to be better.

You're smart.

You have a rejuvenating vibe.

You are gentle.

You are tranquility.

You are special.

(Long pause)

You breathe serenely, you feel that you are in the right place and the perfect moment, you let yourself be carried away by the tender vibes of harmony that wraps you around your feet, tickling up your legs and lodging in your stomach; making you experience a great peace that you have never felt before. You wrap yourself in that emotion, you investigate it and you fully enjoy it. The external discomforts are gone, you have found the direction towards that path you were looking for. Friend, my greatest wish is to help you immerse yourself in inner tranquility that clears up your anguish and thus achieve your rest, but remember that if at any time you feel that you are falling asleep, do not worry, we can meet at another time, let yourself be carried away by your dreams.

(Medium pause)

Now you perceive how your body is getting smaller, you are calm and you enjoy the experience. Your imagination becomes more and more present in you and you begin to feel the place where you are a little warm: there is something white around you with small dark spots, it has an oval shape and you are sitting only admiring that space, there is something in its shape or texture that transports you to your home warmth.

(Short pause)

Suddenly, a soft sound of waves from the sea attracts you and you go towards what seems like a white wall of the place where you are, then you decide to touch it and do it with your index finger three times, which causes it to break easily and break. Make a hole allowing you to look outside. You can see there the immense sea of a dark blue color that dances on the shores of the beach in beautiful turquoise flashes, that image fills you with admiration and you rest your hands on the wall causing it to break and leave you exposed to your new and beautiful around.

(Medium pause)

That shell where you were has said that the time has come for you to come out of it and live every little or great thing in the world, it has opened the doors of your new beginning, it has helped you to be strong and calm in life, that is your great virtue. You are sitting on pieces of that blanket on the soothing white sand. The sky is beginning to clear and the small rays of the sun appear to paint it a beautiful yellow, orange, and pink, you take a deep breath inhaling all the beautiful vibes that nature gives you and then you expel the air with gratitude to the earth and you for allowing yourself that moment.

(Medium pause)

Now you feel by your side the most serene, innocent, and sweet energy that only you are the lucky one to live. A small and tender sea turtle is next to you, he is as impressed by his new world as you are, the two of them look to the horizon imagining the immense world of possibilities, and then they meet each other with their gaze. You are reflected in the big and round eyes of the baby turtle and you find in it your being, your path, the answers, and tranquility, you feel satisfied and happy with who you are, where you are, and what you have.

(Medium pause)

A gentle wave invites them to enter it and gives way to start their new path. You get distracted by seeing how many turtles walk quickly towards the ocean and you notice that among them is also the one you identified with, however, you notice that it stops on the shore, it is waiting for you, it is time to take your first step. . And then you do it, you walk to where your little friend awaits you, you go with your head up and the confidence of what you want. You immerse yourself in the relaxing and loving sea and you are sinking in its sweet waves of sleep, your body is in harmony and your mind is in peace, we have already reached your destination. Rest my friend.

The Secret of Nature

Welcome friend. In this meeting, you and I will go for a walk on a special path, where peace, harmony, and balance are everywhere. You are a majestic being, full of unconditional love, optimism, and full health. Always keep in mind that you deserve the best, and that is why this place that I have created for you, I will help you reprogram your mind by connecting with well-being and letting your senses guide you on this special journey. Here there is no fear or worry, you just have to listen.

(Short pause)

The first thing you will do is looking for a comfortable and serene place where your body feels calm and can flow with the positive energies that surround it. If you want to place yourself in the comfort of your room it will be much better. The place should be cool and serene, away from very loud noises or people who may interfere. Slowly you place yourself on the comfortable surface, where your body can relax. Rest your back on the nice mattress making your head and neck relax. Get into a position where your arms release all the load they are accumulating. When you feel ready, start by closing your eyes and let yourself be carried away by the sound of my voice. The time has come to begin this magnificent journey.

(Short pause)

Inhale slowly, letting the oxygen circulate through your beautiful lungs filling them with revitalizing energies, then exhale slowly and feel how the energy of your heart connects with the energy of the Universe naturally. Your blood travels through your body from the tips of your feet to your heart in a unique way. All your senses begin to function naturally, letting your mind begin to empty itself of all the thoughts that once overwhelmed it. Your soul begins to awaken, flooding you with unequaled hope. Inhale very calmly, and then exhale everything that bothers you, freeing yourself of all your fears. If at any point you feel sleep taking over, don't worry. You just let your body and mind flow.

(Short pause)

Every time you are freeing yourself from everything that disturbs your tranquility. You breathe gently, holding the air in your lungs for a few seconds, letting the positive energies invade your being, and then exhale serenely. Your whole mind is becoming calm, you perceive new and revitalizing sensations; the climate that surrounds you is pleasant; you don't feel any discomfort and everything around you starts to disappear. At this very moment, your consciousness is rising and your body is feeling it. You are doing very well, you are opening yourself to positive energies and leaving behind everything that was disturbing your peace. The dream has taken hold of you, there are no longer thoughts, resistance, or doubts. You're free.

(Short pause)

Every part of you is perfect.

Everything's fine.

You are a wonderful being.

You are the most beautiful light in the Universe.

You are physically and mentally balanced.

You are brave.

You are abundant.

Everything you love with love, you get.

You are an essential part of the beauty of life.

Every moment of your life is perfect and unique.

The love of your soul floods every cell of your body.

Every day is a new opportunity for you to be happy.

(Long pause)

A state of pure relaxation begins to run through your entire body, from your legs to your back. Let your body fall completely on the surface that protects you. Take a deep breath and enjoy this moment with yourself. Feel your body and mind become one with the Universe, and then breathe out freely. You are making way for those healing energies that will reconnect you with well-being and happiness. Focus on the perfect sound originating from your heart. Feel how the air goes through your lungs and caresses everything inside you. A state of satisfaction and calm floods you, freeing you of all the negative that your mind kept.

(Short pause)

A soft and delicate wind caresses your feet, slowly rises your legs, touches your hands, and finally reaches your face. Above you is a beautiful sky, a perfect blue color. The clouds are walking near you and if you raise your hands you can touch them. Beneath your back is a comfortable surface, much like a rug. Your hands caress the grass that is on the ground, it is velvety and has a completely green color. Your mind is in complete tranquility, you feel happy to be in the here and now.

(Short pause)

Everything around you is full of fantastic energy. Your feet can feel the softness of the earth under them. Your soul begins to feel grateful to be in front of this landscape. On the horizon, you can see a huge volcano. It is a majestic and imposing natural beauty in front of everything that surrounds it. Your body just lets itself go and floats like a cloud towards him.

(Short pause)

You continue your relaxing and warm walk. You delight in the wonderful place in front of your eyes, and you thank the Universe for allowing you to be here. A few steps from the great volcano you find a small dresser placed on the floor. Slowly, you sit on it and begin to observe the enormous wonder before you. You detail everything related to it, you visualize how the clouds move around all its surroundings as if together they danced in the company of the wind. You feel how its powerful energy begins to travel your body, vibrating in perfect harmony with that wonderful volcano.

(Short pause)

From where you are, your soul and nature communicate. They remind you of the importance of your existence and nature in the Universe. Take a deep breath, letting the universal energy flow through your entire body, and then exhale. Today this great volcano sits in front of you, to fill you with well-being and harmony so that all your energies are balanced and you can shine.

(Middle pause)

Little by little, you are sinking into the beautiful green grass. You feel like he's gently hugging you, making you relax completely. Your body feels all the energy of the place, wrapping itself in a command of peace and happiness. You feel your body slowly melt onto the mattress, causing you to finally fall asleep. Good night. Dear friend.

Floating alongside the Universe

Welcome friend. In this meeting, you will dedicate that special moment that you deserve so much. You and I will start an amazing adventure, full of calm, optimism, and balance. You are a majestic, unique, and irreplaceable being, capable of achieving everything you want. For that reason. Today you will make your mind fill with what you long for: a deep, calm, and restful sleep. Here in this place, you will recharge your energies, freeing yourself from all those negative thoughts, this guilt that bothers you, you will fill yourself with well-being and positive energy.

(Short pause)

First, you should find a quiet and peaceful place, where you can quiet your thoughts and your body can remain calm. If you wish, it can be in the comfort of your sofa or the warmth of your room. The site must be cool and with good air circulation. Slowly, lie down on the soft bed, rest your head on a cushion or a quilt where you feel more comfortable, making sure that your neck begins to relax, and then place your hands and legs in a position where it is easy for you to release them from tension. , the one that is most pleasant for you. When you feel that everything is ready, close your eyes slowly and allow yourself to be guided easily by my words. It is time to start our journey.

(Short pause)

Inhale slowly, feeling how positive energies fill your lungs, then exhale all those charges that do not let you be free. Notice how your chest moves to the rhythm of your breathing, become aware of every part of you. All your thoughts are flowing, letting go of your fears and worries. The resistances begin to give way, they disappear on their own. Inhale gently, letting the air flow through each space in your lungs for a few seconds, then exhale. If you feel that fatigue begins to take hold of you and you cannot continue, do not worry: you just allow yourself to flow and be one with the Universe. You deserve everything you lovingly desire, you deserve a full rest.

(Short pause)

Everything that is around you, begins to disappear. You are disconnecting from reality. You breathe slowly, exhale little by little. Your mind goes to a place where everything is pleasant and there are no fears or tensions. Right now, your body and spirit are separating. Your mind begins to fill with a warm and embracing light, which heals whatever pain you may be feeling. Your muscles are easing. You feel like your hips, your abdomen, and your neck are flooded by a sensation of well-being. Your heart maintains its natural rhythm and is filled with security.

(Short pause)

Your whole being vibrates in full abundance.

You are divine perfection.

You are the endless source of prosperity.

Every day you successfully achieve everything you want.

You transmit peace and harmony.

You are the healing of your life.

Your being attracts everything positive in the Universe.

You are a divine creation.

You are the most beautiful in the Universe.

You are one with universal energy.

Infinite love invades every cell of your body.

The Universe blesses every step you take.

(Long pause)

A relaxing tingling begins to rise, slowly towards your neck. The weight of your body has completely disappeared on the surface. You are letting yourself be carried away by tranquility, you are surrendering to the desire to rest. Well-being runs through your back, your neck, and finally settles in your mind. Your consciousness begins to awaken, moving to a different plane, the dream is taking over you. There is no resistance, the fears are gone and the pain no longer exists. You find yourself floating in the infinite Universe.

(Short pause)

A breeze fresh caresses all your skin, running through your legs, your hands, your chest, and your cheeks. Above you is a perfect sky full of shining stars. You can notice that each one has a special shine, some are multicolored and others are unicolor. Beneath your back, a velvety surface embraces you: it is a pink cloud. Now you are floating in it. You discover how satisfying it is to feel safe, let your soul surrender completely to this magnificent experience.

(Short pause)

The cloud floats slowly across the sky while you delight in the beautiful brightness of the stars that accompany you on this journey. You see how the other clouds pass by your side, they look soft and comfortable. You feel how the cold of the night runs through your body refreshing you. From where you are, you visualize the entire Universe, in the distance, you can notice the sun, the beautiful moon, and the other planets that are nearby. This Universe is a unique place like you, you feel grateful for living this experience and being able to visualize this wonderful place.

(Short pause)

Little by little, you feel how you begin to descend from the heights. Every cell in your body has relaxed, you let yourself be carried away by the universal energy and all the wonderful things it has in store for you. You watch as huge mountains begin to appear around you, you feel like they take care of your well-being and protect you from all evil. You keep going down until it falls on a comfortable bush, you feel how the trees begin to warm you, and you are filled with pure and incomparable heat. From where you are, you can hear all the sounds of the place: the song of the birds and the rhythm of the waves of the sea crashing with the rocks. Everything is perfect here and now.

(Short pause)

The cloud begins to float and joins you completely. You feel how your soul begins to light up, filling with harmony and hope. The wonderful Universe allows you to join it and heal everything that does not allow you to remain calm. This journey allows you to reconnect with yourself and with the universal energy source. Breathe, little by little, enjoying all the energy that flows in you, exhale, and let yourself go.

(Middle pause)

Slowly you are sinking into the softness of the beautiful pink cloud. Your skin feels the sight again, making you relax even more. Your whole feeling free and full, floating in a cloud of peace and harmony. You feel like you are becoming one with the mattress that supports your body, finally managing to fall asleep completely. Good night. Dear friend.

With a Great Friend

Welcome friend. Today we will have a new meeting, where together we will start a wonderful journey. We immerse ourselves in a sea of positive energies, full of optimism and good vibes. Today you can balance all your senses by filling yourself with all that light that you thought was lost. I am here to help you make sure that you can take a moment for yourself, allowing you to rest from all that noise that does not allow you to get calm: Today your mind and your body connect with abundance and love, freeing you of all tensions and thoughts negatives that may be running through your mind.

(Short pause)

To continue with our meeting, the first thing you will do is find a comfortable and quiet place, where your body can flow with the energy of the Universe. If it is in the comfort of your bed, much better. The place should be cool and away from any noise. Gradually lie down on a comfortable surface or a soft sofa, where your body can completely relax. Rest your back on the soft mattress making your shoulders and head relax. Get into a position where your arms feel relieved. When you are ready, close your eyes slowly and let my voice guide you. It is time to begin.

(Short pause)

Breathe slowly, let your lungs fill with new energy, then breathe out gently. Feel the movement of every cell in your body, as your blood runs through every corner and reaches your heart fluidly. Admire the serene rhythm of your heartbeat and how they take over you. All those thoughts that are passing through your mind are slowly disappearing. You are freeing yourself of all those charges that you once felt against you, they do not put up any resistance, and they just go away. Inhale calmly, fill yourself with positive energies, hold the air in your lungs for a few moments, then exhale and free yourself from everything. If at some point you feel sleep taking over, and you are too tired to continue, no problem. You just let your body and mind relax.

(Short pause)

You are freeing yourself from everything, inhale gently and exhale little by little. Your mind is becoming calm. You feel pleasant sensations that you had not experienced before; the climate is pleasant and your body does not feel any discomfort. Right now, your soul is rising, and you can feel it. Together we are going in the right direction. You are doing it very well. You feel how your feet are relaxing little by little, the tranquility takes hold of you, runs through your legs and your back. Focus on how the air moves in and out of your body, caressing your soft lungs. You are willing to let yourself go, you feel a tingling run through your hip and rise until it runs down your back. Your body and your consciousness are separated, the dream has taken over. There are no thoughts, no resistance. You are free and unattached.

(Middle pause)

You are love.

You are light.

Your whole being is tranquility.

You are pure happiness.

You deserve everything you want and more.

You are one with the Universe.

You are unique and valuable.

You are being free.

You shine with unique and special light.

You're a wonderful person.

You are a perfect, pure, and complete being.

(Long pause)

Full relaxation is taking over you which runs through your arms and your neck. Your body is gently falling on the surface of the mattress. Your whole being is letting go, surrendering to deep sleep and the restorative energies of the Universe. You feel how your tongue begins to weigh, your jaw relaxes and your eyelids weigh more and more until finally, that tranquility reaches your mind. All resistance is gone, your body is light. The dream has taken you to a new place, without doubts or worries.

(Short pause)

A warm breeze caresses your feet, your legs, your hands, and your cheeks. Above you there is a beautiful sky full of blue and pink tones, the sun is on the horizon, greeting you from afar when you see you. Beneath your back is a velvety surface, you feel like you could melt into it. With your hands you caress it and it is a beautiful green grass that welcomes you. You feel confident, full of security and your whole being is connecting with the energies of the Universe.
(Short pause)
The air around you is charged with well-being. In front of you, there is a beautiful path full of huge pine trees and flowers of all colors. You can delight yourself with the delicious aroma that floods the place. Your feet feel the softness of the grass, and your soul is recharged with positive energies. Inhale calmly, appreciating everything you see, then exhale. The place is magical, as you walk along the path, you see how a bear joins the tour, and it has a honey-colored mane and blue eyes like the sky. You feel calm and confident walking alongside him.
(Short pause)

You continue walking and enjoying everything in front of you, together with your great companion. At the end of the path you are at the top of a mountain, you breathe slowly, observing the wonderful view before you and feeling how your being is filled with harmony, and then you exhale. Next to the great bear, you take a seat on the soft earth. He stands next to you and offers you to lie on him. Your hands caress its soft fur and you feel like you are filling with well-being. The powerful energy that emanates also runs through your body, you feel how you vibrate in tune with your new friend.

(Short pause)

From your place, you understand who the big bear is at your side and who you are. This wonderful being next to you is full of universal light, his spirit is the source of perfect wisdom. Today he sits in front of you to give you his tranquility and calm so that you can renew all your energies. Breathe calmly and slowly release all the negative that accompanies you.

(Short pause)

Slowly, you are sinking into the deep blue of the sky. You feel how the gentle breeze caresses your skin, relaxing you even more. Your body floats to a place full of peace and well-being. You feel how your body is completely melting on the mattress and finally, you manage to fall completely asleep. Good night. Dear friend.

A Beautiful Walk on the Sand

Welcome friend. How pleasant it is to receive you here, means that you are managing to balance your energy in the way you want. Today, you and I will immerse ourselves in a river of pleasant emotions, full of peace, love, and trust. You are a wonderful being, full of infinite light, strength, and many good vibes, so you deserve to take a break and dedicate it to yourself, your well-being, and your mind. Your being will connect with that feeling of happiness and abundance that once accompanied you in the course of your life. All tension will disappear, your mind will be free, and fears.

(Short pause)

Before continuing, you should first find a calm and serene place where you feel comfortable. It should be a place where your mind can let go and your body enjoys the moment. Ideally, it should be a place where the air has good circulation and is free from loud sounds. Lean slowly over a bed or a comfortable sofa, place your head on a soft pad, letting your neck begin to relax, let your arms and legs stretch freely. Get into a comfortable position, where tensions ease off peacefully. When you are ready, slowly close your eyes and let yourself be carried away by my voice. It is the moment to dream.

(Short pause)

Inhale keeping the natural rhythm of your being, and then exhale. Start to disconnect from everything around you. Feel the harmonious beat of your heart in the center of your chest. You are leaving aside all those dense thoughts that are passing through your mind, your senses continue to function, operating under their laws and natural forms. You feel freer, those burdens that you had are disappearing, without putting up resistance, they are leaving. Breathe tranquility, and exhale all those negative energies that are still out there, and free yourself from any mental ties. If you start to feel too tired to continue and sleep takes over, no problem: You just have to listen and let your mind relax.

(Short pause)

You feel like everything is disappearing. Inhale gently, filling yourself with well-being, and exhale fully. Your mind is becoming empty, visualize how the Universe begins to embrace you; the climate is pleasant and they feel less and less concerned. In these moments your consciousness begins to rise, you feel it in every space of you. Today we are heading to the right place; you are doing very well, my good friend. You feel how your body relaxes, calm and tranquility are installed in your whole being. You are gently letting yourself be carried away by this sacred moment. You are feeling how your back relaxes completely and that feeling is ascending to your head. Your mind is isolating itself, free from ties and fears.

(Short pause)

Your whole being is full of calm.

You're amazing.

You deserve to recover all those lost energies.

You are love.

You flow like the wind.

You are brave.

Your whole body is completely healthy.

You and the Universe are one.

You are a very strong person.

You are very successful.

Everything you want you can fulfill.

You have a free spirit.

(Long pause)

Your whole being is surrendering to deep sleep and relaxation takes over your mind. You feel a delicate breeze passing through every pore of your skin, running through your legs, your torso, your arms, and finally your face. Breathe calmly and release the air slowly. Above you is a wonderful sky full of orange and reddish tones, you can see in the distance how the sun is hiding through the thin horizon, welcoming a bright and beautiful moon. She shelters you with her warm glow. Beneath your back, a smooth and soft surface makes you aware of where you are. You notice how your soul is full of security, connecting with the Universe. Your body is completely carried away and you feel grateful for this moment.

(Short pause)

Your whole body feels the energy that invades the place, you can see how the sky is filling with small sparkles, surrounding you from the top. You can hear the subtle sound of the ocean waves as they roll across the sand. The refreshing breeze moves across your skin, providing you with peace and satisfaction. Inhale calmly and exhale slowly. Before you visualize a huge beach, which seems to have no end, it is calm and serene. As you move forward you realize that it is a charming place, you feel like the paradise before you thank you that you are in the here and now.

(Short pause)

As you continue advancing, you can see a magical flame on the shore of the beach. Something in the depths of your being is responding to its call and without realizing it your feet begin to float in that direction. Inhale slowly and exhale, always maintaining your natural rhythm. You are not afraid, your soul is full of confidence and security. Upon reaching the shore, the flame is placed in front of you. It has a purple color and when you approach it you feel like it is filling you with maximum fullness. The powerful energy that emanates from it begins to travel throughout your body, making you vibrate in tune with the Universe.

(Short pause)

The purple flame begins to embrace you. Your soul begins to heal, from the most superficial to the deepest of your being. This wonderful light before you is the source of universal healing and well-being. Today it appears before you to give you all the calm and happiness that you needed, thus renewing all your energies so that from this moment your light does not go out. Breathe calmly, keeping the air in your lungs, and then slowly release everything that is no longer working in your thoughts.

(Middle pause)

Slowly you sink into that deep purple flame. A gentle wind caresses your face, relaxing you much more. Your body is floating through the sea full of peace and well-being. Your energy becomes one with the Universe. You feel how you melt into the mattress that supports you and finally, you manage to fall completely asleep. Good night. Dear friend.

An Oasis to Dream

I welcome you back, friend. I am glad to know that you liked our meditating sessions. That means that you have managed to achieve that calm that you wanted so much. In this new encounter, you and I will go on a magnificent journey where silence, peace, and harmony will accompany us. Keep in mind that you are a unique being, filled with the brightest light in the Universe. You deserve that your body, your soul, and your mind are aligned with the universal unit. This space is dedicated to you, to help you get that rest that you long for. Today the noise of your thoughts will disappear, leaving your mind to feel free and calm.

(Short pause)

Before continuing with our meeting, you must locate a comfortable and serene place, where silence can accompany us and your body can flow with universal wisdom. If you like it in the comfort of your bedroom, no problem, however, I suggest the place should be away from annoying sounds and be as cool as possible so that your body relaxes completely. Lay your back on a soft surface, managed to place yourself in the right position so that you release all the tensions that accompany you. Let your arms and legs break free. When you are ready, close your eyes and trust my voice. The time has come to begin.

(Short pause)

Slowly allow your lungs to be embraced by the air that goes through it, then exhale letting yourself go. Be aware of the movement that your chest exerts when you breathe, feel how it rises and falls. The melody of your heartbeat takes over you and makes you feel like the blood runs through each space of you. Your mind begins to empty, leaving it free and unburdened. All your resistances are gone, the fears and insecurities are gone. Inhale gently, filling yourself with security and peace, hold the air for a few seconds in your lungs, then exhale and release everything that no longer belongs to you.

(Short pause)

Your being feels it, you are freeing yourself from everything. Inhale little by little and then exhale, maintaining the natural rhythm of your body. Calm is taking over your mind, you begin to experience new sensations. The climate begins to change, now it is more pleasant and everything you had around you is gone. You are doing very well, my good friend. You deserve to reconnect with the Universe and be one with it. You feel the calm taking over your feet and your legs. A feeling of peace and harmony takes over you, running through your chest and arms. Focus on everything that you are experiencing. Today you are willing to let yourself be carried away by sleep and relaxation. Now you feel like that sensation runs down your back until it ends in your head. There are no resistances, no ties. Here and now you are free.

(Short pause)

You are a magnet for fortune.

You are pure energy.

You are the owner of your life.

Success is inevitable in your life.

You are abundant.

Your whole being is full of confidence.

Every day you are stronger.

You have creative power in your hands.

Your whole being is unique and unrepeatable.

You are grateful to the Universe.

You are on the right track.

(Long pause)

Full relaxation is already a part of you, your body falls completely on the surface that huddles it. Your whole being is surrendering to a deep and revitalizing sleep. The energies begin to align and the Universe is perfectly balanced. Inhale and exhale calmly. Your limbs begin to think and you feel how your consciousness is separating from your physical form. The dream begins to take over you and takes you to a special place, where there are only well-being and harmony.

(Short pause)

A smooth surface caresses your hands and supports your entire body. Above you is a wonderful dark sky, decorated with an infinity of stars. The moon welcomes you with love, making me feel part of the place. Little by little you sit down, look around you and notice the beautiful desert before you. The place is full of huge palm trees and small cacti. With your hands, you can feel the delicacy of the sand. You feel happy, full of security, and with immense peace.

(Short pause)

The breeze that moves around you is full of peace. In the distance, you can see a beautiful oasis full of palm trees and desert flowers. The deepest part of your soul recognizes the place, response to its call and your feet set off, heading for the place. Inhale the scent of the night and exhale all the negative that remains in your mind. From where you are you enjoy the landscape, you delight in the softness of the sand under your feet and the company of the radiant moon that decorates the night sky. You feel alive and every pore of your skin is filled with harmony.

(Short pause)

You continue walking through the place until you reach the wonderful paradise. The water of the oasis is crystal clear, the palm trees that are around it begin to dance with the gentle rhythm of the wind and you can hear the pleasant sound of their leaves when they move. At that point, a small firefly appears and shyly approaches you, landing on your fingers. When it touches you, an immense light begins to come out of it. Hugging me completely. The magical energy of the firefly begins to heal you, filling you with harmony and well-being.

(Middle pause)

The light that embraces you immerses you in a deep state of happiness. You feel how the night breeze touches your skin, making you relax many more. Your body floats and maintains a calm state. You have the feeling of well-being running through your entire being. Slowly your body becomes one with it with the mattress where you are and finally, you manage to fall deeply asleep. Good night. Dear friend.

A Journey through the Beautiful Horizon

Hello dear friend, I welcome you to this magnificent meeting. Together we will immerse ourselves in a sea of positive energies. I will show you how good it feels to connect with the harmony and peace of the Universe. You are a unique being, full of love and well-being. You deserve that your mind the tranquility of your mind and all the abundance that you desire. This space is for you so that you can calm your mind of all those fears that afflict you and do not let you continue. Today you will redirect your attention to full rest. The negative thoughts are gone, your mind is becoming empty and silent.

(Short pause)

To start our great adventure, you must find a pleasant and pleasant place, allowing your body to flow with universal energy. It can be in the comfort of your favorite sofa or your bed much better. The place must have a fresh atmosphere, where silence is our best companion. Slowly lie down on the pleasant surface, allowing your whole body to relax. Drop your back onto the soft mattress making your shoulders relax. Your arms and legs should be in a position where you can release all the tensions they carry. When you feel ready, close your eyes and let me guide you. It is time to start.

(Short pause)

Take a deep breath, feel how your lungs recharge with new energy and then release all that weight that your mind accumulates. Feel how your neurons make that wonderful connection with each other and open them to receive the energy of the Universe. Your cells recognize what is happening, they begin to vibrate in perfect harmony to give you the opportunity that you lived a magnificent experience next to the great source. Your mind empties, you do not put any resistance to your thoughts. Inhale gently, fill yourself with positive energies, and then exhale, releasing yourself from everything. If at any moment you feel that sleep takes over you and fatigue does not let you continue, or there is a problem. You just let your body and mind stay calm and relax.

(Short pause)

You feel light, you have freed yourself from everything. Breathe gently and let the air out little by little. Your mind becomes calm. Your body begins to perceive new emotions, the climate is totally pleasant, your body feels grateful and your mind is passing through a space of well-being. Here and now, your soul turns to itself intonation with the Universe, becoming a receiving antenna of love, harmony, balance, and peace. Together we are going in the right direction. You are doing very well, my good friend. You feel a tingling run through your feet and back. Become aware of how air enters your nose and slowly exits your mouth. Today you are willing to flow in the river of positive energy that invades your mind. The tranquility takes hold of you, running down your back until it reaches your neck. The dream is taking over you. There are no fears, no worries. From today you are free to let yourself go and live fully.

(Short pause)

You are a kind person.

You are a being full of infinite light.

You love yourself just the way you are.

You are perfect and you love yourself for it.

You are unconditional love.

Your whole being is full of peace and harmony.

Today you choose to be one with the Universe.

You are full of gratitude.

You deserve everything and each one of the things that you have dreamed of in life.

You are a successful person full of abundance.

You're happy.

(Long pause)

A sense of harmony will it is taking over you, runs through your limbs, and reaches your back. Your body is accommodating itself on the surface that surrounds it. You are letting yourself go, you are indulging in a deep and restful sleep. You feel how your face is feeling heavy, your jaw, and your cheeks feel completely relaxed. There are no resistances, no dangers. Your body begins to lighten up. The Dream is taking you to a majestic place, where there are only well-being and harmony.

(Short pause)

A gentle breeze caresses your skin, running through every part of you. The sky before you is loaded with orange and yellow hues, reflecting a beautiful sunset. The sun is at the midpoint of the horizon and the weather around you is perfect. Below you is a smooth surface, with your hands, you caress it and appreciate the moment that the landscape is giving you. Your whole feeling safe, confident, and in balance.

(Short pause)

In front of you is a huge pink hot air balloon. Slowly, you step into it and start it up. A tropical smell takes over your nostrils and when you notice it you are floating above a beautiful crystalline beach. Your hair dances under the gentle wind and your fingers play with the clouds that are approaching you. The place is magical, you feel how your soul begins to absorb all the energies that surround the globe and you enjoy the wonderful view. Inhale calmly, and exhale everything that bothers you. As you follow the route, you visualize a beautiful cliff. Where the sea collides with the roses and a light aroma of salt takes over the place.

(Short pause)

As you float through the air, the beautiful landscapes do not stop appearing. You see wonderful mountains, valleys, and rivers, which add to the source of divine energy. You breathe in slowly and exhale everything that no longer vibrates with you. From that place where you are, the Universe is in charge of communicating with your soul and you feel it inside you. Little by little you get closer to the last ray that the sun gives you before setting and that ray connects you with the most powerful source that exists.

(Short pause)

You understand your place in the Universe, your being is filled with gratitude and pure love. Slowly, you are sinking into that ray of harmonious light that the sun has given you. Your body begins to float, it is flooded with well-being and complete tranquility. You feel like your body has fully integrated into the mattress and finally, you manage to fall asleep completely. Good night. Dear friend.

A Magical Waterfall

Welcome, dear friend. In this meeting, you and I will start a magical journey where you can recharge yourself with positive energies. Together we will take a walk through a wonderful place, full of harmony, love, and happiness. You are a special being, full of unique and incomparable essence. You are worthy of the well-being of your body and your mind. These seconds that you will dedicate will be the best, they will help you redirect your thoughts towards what you have wanted so much: Rest and deep sleep. All the negative disappears, emptying your mind of everything that worries you and filling it with peace.

(Short pause)

To continue with our tour, you must find a quiet and comfortable place, where you can experience the incredible opportunity to be totally at peace. It must be a space without noise or disturbances. May it help you to enjoy the silence, not only in the physical sense but also in the depths of your mind? The best thing is that it is a place where the air can flow easily, with a cool and pleasant environment for you. Slowly place your head on a comfortable surface, allowing the tensions in your neck to disappear, let your arms join the comfort, relaxing them little by little. When you're ready, close your eyes and trust the sound of my voice. The time has come to start dreaming.

(Short pause)

Breathe in, little by little, and then exhale. Allowing you to recognize everything that happens within you. Feel the absolute vibration of each cell of your body, the balanced melody of your heartbeat is taking over you, keep your mind serene and calm. All negative thoughts are left out of you, in the depths of your being your soul begins to awaken and warns you that it is time to flow with it. You breathe in tranquility and breathe out everything that does not let you be free. If you feel that fatigue takes hold of you and sleep does not let you continue, calm down, no problem. Just let yourself be carried away by my voice and flow like the wind.

(Short pause)

Everything around you is gone. Inhale slowly, at the rhythm of the Universe, and then exhale little by little. Your mind is balancing, there are no more fears, and there is only safety and love in this space. The climate that surrounds you is satisfactory, each time you feel lighter and carefree. Here and now your body and mind begin to separate. Your body relaxes more and more, tranquility and balance are part of you. You are letting yourself go. Your limbs and your back are completely relaxed, your mind flows with the universal energy, feeling free and without problems.

(Short pause)

You are a complete, wonderful, and perfect person.

Everything wonderful is attached to you.

You shine with the universal light.

Everything you want the Universe gives you.

You are surrounded by love.

It has a unique essence.

You deserve all the best in the world and you accept it with open arms.

Everything you need is within you.

The Universe embraces you with its unconditional love.

You are a special being.

You are a loving and full being.

(Long pause)

All the resistances have disappeared, a relaxation is beginning to take hold of you, and it runs through your legs and your hips until it reaches your back. You are letting yourself be calm, indulging in deep and restful sleep. Your neck and face feel relieved. Your whole beginning to recharge with the best energies of gratitude and hope. There are no thoughts anymore, there is only you and me. Here you don't have to worry, you just have to trust.

(Short pause)

A velvety breeze caresses your skin, runs through your feet, your hands, and finally your face. You can see a wonderful blue sky, around you are a large number of trees covered with flowers. Your feet enjoy a smooth surface and a pleasant tropical aroma that runs throughout the place fills your nostrils. You feel full, full of security and pure love. Your soul connects with well-being and tranquility.

(Short pause)

On the horizon, you can see a path decorated with wine-colored flowers. The whole place is wonderful, your feet enjoy contact with the earth, your mind is in balance and your being is recharged with positive energies. Breathe calmly, detailing everything around you. And then exhale. At the end of the path, you see a beautiful threshold that welcomes you, when you cross it before you a majestic waterfall is shown. Everything is soaked in the energies of the place.

(Short pause)

Little by little you are getting closer. The waterfall reflects the enchanting blue of the sky and around it has gray rocks that balance the landscape. You breathe slowly, visualizing the whole place, then you exhale. As you get closer you notice that in front of her is a wide wooden chair. Your whole body responds to the powerful energies that surround you and little by little you slowly take a seat on the wooden surface. You can feel it with your hands, it is a comfortable surface and gives you the best view of the entire landscape.

(Short pause)

From your place you are grateful to be in the here and now, your soul to understand what nature is and who you are at this moment. This wonderful space in front of you is the perfect cascade of well-being and wisdom that recharges you with everything you thought was lost. Inhale calmly and slowly exhale all the problems that you feel are still with you.

(Middle pause)

Slowly, you sink into the deep waterfall in front of you. Feel how the water begins to travel all over your skin, bathing you in your power, letting your body begin to float towards a place full of tranquility and harmony. Slowly you melt completely onto the mattress and finally, you fall completely asleep. Good night. Dear friend.

The Great Lake that Became my Purpose

Hi friend. It is nice to know that you have decided to take a break in your life and take time to relax. This experience will also allow you from your imagination to live an adventure that will help you improve your rest and your sleep. Also, find calm and tranquility. Feel worthy of this experience that will allow you well-being and health.

(Short pause)

I invite you to find a quiet place, lie down on a bed, place your body straight, stretch little by little and try to feel as comfortable as possible. Relax your neck and try to be free of tension. That will facilitate the processes that we will initiate and you will enjoy more of the benefits of guided relaxation. The chosen place must be free from interference and distractions.

(Short pause)

Close your eyes and take a deep breath. Inhale and exhale gently. If you have any worries or thoughts that bother you, hand them over to the Universe, get rid of them, and don't allow them to steal your energy. Instead of those thoughts, charge your life with positive thoughts that give you a new vibe, so that the energy flows in harmony and peace.

(Short pause)

This experience that you are living is a great opportunity to relax and find the peace and tranquility that you long for. Feel how your body is getting better. Consciously, you are seeking and finding health, harmony, and well-being. That makes you feel good and happy. Think that what you are living is a first step to achieve a new course that will help you lead a healthier life, where your being and your spirit will be in harmony with the Universe.

(Short pause)

Feel that this pause that you are giving your life is necessary, to be able to move forward with other expectations and more encouragement. You must value every day and enjoy each learning experience to the fullest. Do not forget:

You are a being of decisions for your good and strengthening.

You can achieve what you propose for your well-being.

The end is not the goal, but the enjoyment of each step that will allow you to reach the goal.

You will be great, to the extent that you greatly enjoy the small achievements that you are achieving.

(Long pause)

I invite you to introduce yourself to me is this great adventure, if you feel that you do not want to continue because you are sleepy, there is no problem, rest, other days continue. Remember that the purpose of this activity is for you to rest and sleep soundly. So let's start our journey.

(Short pause)

You're traveling to a very special place. You perceive how your body and your sight meet a beautiful landscape. You are on an island looking at a calm beach with no waves on the horizon. You sit on the shore and enjoy the first rays of sunshine of that new day. A gentle breeze caresses your skin and you enjoy the delicate sand where you are sitting. It is a pleasure to be in that place, the contemplation of that natural landscape fills you with many emotions.

(Short pause)

You decide to walk along the seashore, you watch the dance of the small waves that bring water to the shore, and then it returns to join the sea again. That dance relaxes your mind and your spirit. You see how your footprints are being etched on the shore and that makes you think about what you will experience on this wonderful trip. You decide to go to know the interior of the island. You find many palm trees, and trees typical of the area. You see a mountain with abundant vegetation and you feel that you want to go in that direction and you do so.

(Short pause)

As you go up, you feel a cool climate. On the way, you see that there are fruit trees. When you reach the peak of the mountain, you can see a large freshwater lake in the distance. You realize that to get to that place you have to travel a long path. That does not stop you, because that natural beauty is worth the efforts that can be made to see it up close.

(Short pause)

On the way, you see an area full of a variety of cacti. These are very beautiful and perfect, some have beautiful flowers of different colors. You know that you are privileged since this landscape cannot be observed so easily. After carefully observing each of the cactus species, you border the area to continue your journey. You have the feeling that these plants give off a very delicious aroma.

(Short pause)

You breathe deeply and with a certain nostalgia, you leave that place so curiously created by the Universe. Then, you walk little by little and you look at a passage that shows a large bower and you go there. With your hands, you remove part of the vegetation and you will be surprised that you have reached a cliff. As you get closer, you realize that you can observe the sea in its immensity. In that place you stay a while, appreciating how the sea and the sky come together and seem to be one. The shades of blue are very similar, it is not clear where the sky ends or where the sea begins. You thank the Universe for the possibility of seeing this great show that this trip has shown you.

(Short pause)

You decide to continue your adventure, you walk with great enthusiasm since the route is loaded with places, landscapes, challenges, and curiosities that require you to be animated and willing to live each experience. You hear how the water runs down a stream and you decide to find the origin of that sound. You see that the water comes from a small stream, you go over there, wash your face and drink some of the water, which is very crystal clear. You decide to continue along the river bank. You observe that in some places small pools have formed, which store the water and from there, small streams flow that runs through various areas of the place. You can see how the land there is fertile and dark. You enjoy the smell of the place, which is humid and incredibly fresh.

(Short pause)

You hear a loud sound of a great waterfall falling and hitting the stones. You realize that you have reached the great lake you were looking for. You climb some stones and you reach a small flat top, where there are some large trees, which shade the place. You decide to sit on the big roots near the stem of one of them. From there, you capture the movement and energy that is generated in that place. You feel happy to be there and you perceive how small drops splash and wet you. You like the melody of that place where the sounds of falling water and the singing of birds come together. You enjoy having achieved your goal, and for living each step that helped you achieve it. You feel that this journey taught you that you are brave, capable, strong, and a fighter. In these moments you lean on the trunk of the tree that shelters you and you want to rest.

The Great Seat of Silence

Welcome friend. How interesting that today you have decided to dedicate a moment of your time to yourself. I know that maybe making this decision is sometimes complicated, because we have many things to do and we tend to prioritize everything, except to stop and take a break for ourselves, to pamper ourselves, love ourselves, and dedicate ourselves to cultivating our spirit and our soul.

(Short pause)

At this time I invite you to follow my guidelines. Find a quiet place, where you can, with my support, live a guided relaxation experience. Lie down on your bed, make sure your back is straight and that your neck is supported by a soft pillow, so that it relaxes. Seek to be free of distracting tensions so that you can concentrate. (Short pause)

Close your eyes, feel how your body enjoys that moment. You inhale deeply and fill your lungs with air that comes to revitalize your life, then you exhale and let everything that worries you out of you. You become aware in this moment, of your thoughts, emotions, and feelings. If you find that something is disturbing you, release them and hand them over to the Universe. Feel that you are light, that new positive energy recharges your whole being and makes you vibrate in harmony.

(Short pause)

At this moment you feel peace, tranquility, and calm. You perceive yourself as relaxed and you want to always stay that way because that state makes you feel happy, healthy, and cheerful. You understand that you must prioritize your life and dedicate more moments to lift your spirit and heal your body. At that moment you become aware of your heartbeat and your breathing. You are grateful for life and the possibility of having this experience. Internally, you know that:

You are a being of love

You can love and take care of yourself

You need to go inside to achieve peace, the harmony, and well-being you deserve.

Silence helps you to be more aware of your strengths.

(Long pause)

The time has come to start our adventure. For this reason, we must submerge ourselves little by little through our imagination, in a journey that will allow us to find ourselves, relax and be able to rest deeply. If in these moments, you feel sleepy, there are no problems, you can rest, that is part of what is intended with this activity. Another day you can continue.

(Short pause)

Little by little you feel that you are walking up a hill. You look to the sides and see a large mountain range. Feel a cold and delicious climate that runs through your entire body. You perceive the presence of many people walking in the same direction where you are also going. They all wear jackets, hats, and gloves. They also carry backpacks and ice skating shoes. You see a lot of food sales and very provocative smells on the tour. You feel like everyone is in a rush. You decide to go calmly and appreciate everything that this new experience that you are going to live offers you.

(Short pause)

You perceive joy in the environment, and enthusiasm reigns in the place, and that makes you feel happy. You see that you are heading to an immense natural park, where there is a zoo, natural beauties, caves, springs, waterfalls and waterfalls, forests, and also social places such as a skating rink, dance halls, rooms to listen to music, and to read. Also, for the little ones, there are entertainment and a small circus. Upon arrival, you are greeted by some people who are responsible for the place and give you several options from which you choose to have an adventure, which you will do alone and is called: The seat of silence. You receive a map to start your tour and they inform you that you will have support throughout the tour, through visitor orientation points.

(Short pause)

When you start your journey, you see some people who go ahead of you, each one going alone. You appreciate that the path you are walking on is built of cement and has some colored stones embedded in it. On the sides of the road, there are wildflowers of many colors. You notice that every certain distance there are metal benches, painted white, where visitors can sit. On the way, some kinds of tunnels have been formed, because trees on both sides of the road have crossed their branches and a kind of arch has been formed through which visitors pass. In some of these tunnel locations, the trees are in bloom and look beautiful. You enjoy the tour and you marvel at what you find.
(Short pause)

As you walk, the foliage is leafier. It seems that on each side of the road there is a large forest. The trees are getting bigger and older. On the tour, you get to the first visitor orientation point. There they offer you bottled water and a packed snack for your trip. Also, they ask you how you have felt and if you need some guidance. You feel satisfied with the attention and continue your great adventure.

(Short pause)

Little by little, the weather is getting a little colder, you perceive that the mist appears timidly to give your landscape a bit of magic. As you walk, you feel that no noise is heard. Then you start to listen to yourself. You become aware of the sound of your footsteps, your breathing, and the beating of your heart. You find it interesting to feel yourself, to know that you are alive and that you are walking towards a place that will bring learning to your life.

(Short pause)

In this fascinating route you come across an old tree with pink flowers, next to it there is a large lagoon, surrounded by orchids and white lilies. Everything is impregnated with the aroma emanating from the flowers. In that wonderful place, there are some comfortable benches where you sit and lie down. You drink some water and eat the snack you received. Everything there is calm and silent. You feel the harmony and beauty of the place. That pleasant climate makes you find yourself.

(Short pause)

You check then, your thoughts, your feelings and your emotions, which you perceive are in the same harmony of stillness, calm, and tranquility. You thank the Universe for this beautiful experience, for finding yourself in the instructive silence of that wonderful place, and for allowing you to understand the need you have to take time to enjoy the silence and meet your essence and your being, which is worthy of peace, and love. Suddenly you realize that your whole body is crying out for a rest, you lie down on the great seat where you are and sleep soundly.

Dancing in a Sacred Place

I welcome you, friend. It is nice to know that today you thought a bit about yourself and decided to give yourself some time to relax. Through guided meditation and with the implementation of your creativity and imagination we will live an adventure that will bring you calm, well-being, and harmony. Important conditions that will help you to have a good rest and to achieve a pleasant sleep.

(Short pause)

I invite you to find a comfortable and quiet place, where you have privacy. Lie down on your bed. Try that your head is comfortably rested on a soft pillow. Stretch your body and keep your back straight. Your neck should be relaxed and you shouldn't feel any tension. Prepare that place with care so that you feel in a special space, where you will live this beautiful adventure, which will help you restfully.

(Short pause)

Close your eyes breathe gently but deeply. Inhale, and feel the benefits of air as they enter your lungs and then exhale so that you deliver to the Universe everything that should no longer be in you. Empty your mind of all those thoughts that worry you and do not allow you to concentrate. If you have any feelings that agitate you, release them and give them to the Universe so that it can transform it.
(Short pause)

You feel how your body is relaxed, because of the conscious breaths that you have taken and because you have released your loads. You perceive that your body is light and that the healing energies run through all the veins and cells, allowing your being and your spirit to feel fullness and happiness. In this tune, you enjoy how your soul rises and feels free. Energies flow through your body that brings you peace, tranquility, and harmony. From inside you understand that
You are a being of love and commitment to others and yourself.

You deserve to be cared for and loved by you,
Your strengths depend on your inner strength, which
you must enliven and cultivate.
You are a being with a healing capacity.

(Long pause)

We have reached a very important moment in this adventure, where together we will travel through imagination to a wonderful place, where you will have the opportunity to reflect, relax and learn. If when you arrive here, you feel that you are sleepy and do not want to continue, no problem, rest. Remember that the main purpose of this activity is that you achieve rest and pleasant sleep.

(Short pause)

From your imagination, you move to a sacred temple. When you arrive at that place you perceive different energy. Some monks greet you and welcome you. They place you in a very beautiful cabin and give you white clothes, so you can participate in the planned activities. You change your clothes and follow some directions. Then you go to where other visitors are.

(Short pause)

You notice that visitors choose the activities they want to do and the tour guides support them. You choose that you want to learn to dance as the first activity. Therefore, the guides take you to a large room, with a very beautiful and polished floor. You enter the place barefoot, as the instructions indicate. The guides play a melody and indicate that you must listen to it deeply. That only when you understand it is that you can and will want to dance. You sit on the floor and listen deeply, but you cannot feel what the melody wants to convey to you, since you think that it has no rhythm and you also feel that it is not harmonious.

(Short pause)

You decide to lie on the floor to see if that way you can hear her deeply. In that position, you pick up the dominant vibrations of the melody through your whole body and you can identify the rhythm. Your heart feels the beats of the song. You begin to move your feet, from the lying position to the rhythm of the melody. You get up and with gentle movements, you simulate what the song is making you feel. Dances for an hour and a half and this activity makes you feel very good, in a harmony of tranquility, calm, harmony, and well-being. Little by little you leave the place and go to the guides to obtain permission for the next activity.

(Short pause)

You decide to go to the sacred pool. You receive a white towel that the guides give you and they give you the instructions that you must follow to start your sacred bath. Also, they indicate the direction to where that place is. Remember that when you arrive at the entrance, you must take off your shoes and clothes, you can only go wrapped in the towel. You realize that to get to the pool you have to go up some stairs. That whole place is clean and highly polished. In the instructions, they indicate that you must go step by step listening to the melody of the breeze and dancing according to what the breeze makes you feel.

(Short pause)

You follow the indications and a few meters from the entrance, you find yourself dancing softly to the rhythm of the breeze. You feel a wonderful sensation, you flow naturally and you are given the experience, you have confidence and high expectations. When you get to the pool you enter it by going down some steps. The water is crystal clear and warm, you proceed to submerge your head and swim. You become aware of the well-being you feel with the bath you are giving yourself. You feel that this place is truly sacred and it emanates peace, harmony, and calm. You enjoy everything you are receiving and you thank the Universe for living this experience.

(Short pause)

You reflect, there in the pool, of the two activities you have experienced. You question your way of living without really listening to what life and other beings want to tell you. You conclude that it suggests: that everything has its voice and meaning and we must learn to deepen from our hearts what it wants to say to us, the whole that speaks. And that the growth of the human being implies knowing how to listen and interpret in silence. Besides, you understand that dance makes us aware of the language that cannot be expressed with the same human codes, but which are there, to give harmony to the world and to charge the spaces with positive vibes and love.

(Short pause)

You get out of the pool, dry off with the towel and walk towards the exit. There you get dressed and decide to sit in a place where there is a group of palm trees, there the ground is full of very fine dark green grass. You lie down on one of the logs and when you put your head down, you want to sleep. And therewith that beautiful landscape, you rest pleased and happy. Sweet dreams, my good friend.

Happiness and Music

Welcome friend. I celebrate for you because you have allowed yourself to participate in this experience of relaxation, which will help you find calm and pleasant sleep. This decision to dedicate time to yourself and to give yourself a moment to enjoy and feel worthy of experiences that nurture you is necessary to strengthen you and fill you with new energy to move forward, with new expectations and encouragement.

(Short pause)

Now he invited you to pay attention to the indications that I am going to offer you. You must be in a pleasant and quiet space. Get into your bed and lie down in a comfortable position, make sure your back is straight. Stretch your body and relax your neck. Seek to be free of tension. It is necessary that during this activity you do not have interferences or interruptions. In this way, you will concentrate better and enjoy the experience.

(Short pause)

Close your eyes become aware of your thoughts. Empty those that prevent you from concentrating, those that distract and worry you. Surrender all your concerns to the Universe and ask for new energies that allow you to flow in harmony, peace, and tranquility. Free from those thoughts, breathe deeply, and thank the Universe for being in the here and now, open to learning, willing to relax and find the rest you so deserve.

(Short pause)

Remember that this break that you have given yourself will allow you to relax and find peace. One of the purposes of this activity is that you can find yourself, value yourself, love yourself, and have a place for yourself to look at new horizons and heal any situation that could be affecting your being and your spirit. Feel worthy of happiness, health, and love. Activate your imagination and open yourself to the opportunity to grow and achieve your well-being.

(Short pause)

You need to become aware of how valuable you are. Feel that you are worthy of all the good that the

Universe has for you. Be ready to receive health, prosperity, peace, harmony, love, friendship, and well-being. You must always remember that:

You deserve to be happy.

You're a wonderful human being.

A being of light capable of loving others.

But mainly love yourself.

That is why you are healthy, loved, happy, and well-being being.

(Long pause)

Now, I invite you to start this journey with me, immerse yourself in the depth of your imagination. If you feel like sleeping, no problem, you can. Remember that this is the end of this journey. Now, you can rest and relax.

From your heart, you decide to give yourself a wonderful adventure where you aspire to feel happy. Therefore, you travel from your imagination many places. On that road, you stop to look at a very beautiful town, which grabs you for the energy you manage to feel. You listen from the nooks and crannies of that place to various melodies from various string and wind instruments. You start your walk in the narrow streets of that town, where all the houses are designed in a particular way, none have fences, all are painted with cheerful colors and in each garden, there are roses, tuberose, orchids, dahlias, and tulips.

(Short pause)

You notice that in many houses there are workshops, where they make instruments. You see children, youth, and adults practicing with them. You catch school to teach music. You see people gathered playing songs together, with various instruments. The atmosphere of happiness that is breathed in that town because of the music, seems wonderful to you.

(Short pause)

You decide to visit a workshop and capture the mystique and love, with which they build each piece. Besides, you perceive that the artisans take care of all the details so that each instrument is a work of art, not only in its shape but also in the sound that they are going to produce when they are played. You perceive their happiness and pride at the end of work. You reflect on the importance of caring for the environment and the strategies to achieve happiness and you realize that mysticism and love are ingredients of it. You understand that by being happy you want everyone to be happy, that is why your behavior must transmit the essence of love and act correctly.

(Short pause)

You go to one of the music schools and observe the teacher's friendly and respectful treatment of his apprentices and the way they seek to make them fall in love with music. Apprentices enjoy training because they receive more than just information. You see how the teachers make the apprentices understand that music is a gift and a good that must be cultivated and loved. You understand that music must be learned, fostered and that it is part of the integral development of the being. Happiness, as well as music, are part of being, but it must be learned and cultivated, not as an end but as part of life and as an attitude towards life.

(Short pause)

Then you approach various groups that perform songs and melodies and see signs of happiness in creating, by achieving team and solo production, flawless melodies, and tunes. You appreciate that happiness is achieved when goals are achieved together or alone. But, it is important to note that even if the goal is not achieved in the planned time, each advance brings happiness and joy. You understand that those moments of happiness have to be enjoyed and lived deeply because they feed the spirit and the soul.

(Short pause)

While on that adventure, you find out that on the night of that day, there will be a great festival, which takes place every year, where all the groups of the town will participate. That excites you and you want to participate. You hear very beautiful songs in the distance and you decide to go see what it is about. You catch that the melody is coming from a church and you get closer. There you observe a choir of children, who at a very young age have learned to play various instruments and other children who sing. At that moment, you feel the happiness that this group of boys transmits with their interpretation and the beautiful energy that they spread to the parishioners.

(Short pause)

You attend the great festival and to your surprise, the opening activity of the festival brings together all the musicians of the town. Children, youth, adults, and the elderly. You consider it to be the most beautiful thing your eyes have seen. With that memory, you leave the place and reflect on the importance of learning to transmit to the values and customs of the new generations that contribute to the happiness of all. Little by little your imagination takes you home, you feel that you are getting tired and you need to recharge your batteries. You are grateful for what you have experienced and your eyes close on their own, giving you a deep and peaceful sleep. Good night.

Inner Strength

Welcome friend. I congratulate you, today you have made an important decision for your life. You have given a break from your usual activities, to dedicate a little time to your being. With this activity, you will have a guided meditation that will allow you to relax, achieve a pleasant sleep and find the calm you long for. Success and enjoy this experience that will take you from your imagination to a special place, where you will learn and meet.

(Short pause)

I invite you at this time, to find a quiet place without interference. Lie down on your bed, straighten your back, stretch your body, relax your neck, and release any distracting tension. Place a soft pillow under your head, allowing you to be comfortable. Feel that that place where you are will allow you to find harmony and tranquility. (Short pause)

(Short pause)

You close your eyes, take control of your thoughts and feelings. You empty your mind of all those thoughts that worry you, give them to the Universe. You breathe deeply. As you inhale, you feel the positive and healing energies enter your body to relax you and give you well-being. When you exhale, you perceive how everything you no longer need comes out of you. You feel that your body is light and without loads.

(Short pause)

In these moments you feel relaxed and at peace. You become aware of the importance of staying with the positive vibe because you rise and perceive life differently. You feel the health in your life and your spirit, and that gives you a lot of happiness. You realize that throughout your body, healing energies are present. You thank the Universe for allowing you to be in that tune. Internally you know that:

Your inner strength is there within you, waiting for you.

You are responsible for achieving harmony, peace, and calm in your life.

You can rise above difficulties and be happy.

(Long pause)

It is time to start our journey together, for this immerse yourself in the depths of your imagination to move to that beautiful place where teachings and good energies await you. If you feel that you are sleepy and you cannot continue, no problem, you can do it another day. Remember that the main purpose of this activity is that you achieve rest and pleasant sleep.

(Short pause)

You feel your body slide down a slide. When you fall you arrive at a beautiful park. There are swings and trains for the little ones. You look at the different attractions that this site offers, they appear in a large list, referring to the natural beauties and the diversions that are promoted there. You read carefully, and you realize that one of the attractions is related to Looking for your inner strength. From your heart, you feel that it wants to go there. You buy a ticket and receive the instructions to make the excursion to the selected site.

(Short pause)

You feel spirited and you walk determined to know the place, you have high expectations. However, you realize that you already have more than an hour and you have followed all the instructions, but you have not reached your destination. You decide then to sit on the shore of a small stream. In this one, you see small golden and raised fish. You appreciate that there are colored pebbles at the bottom of the stream. There are small snails and tiny crabs. Then you turn around when you see the path you left behind and you think, maybe you missed many good moments like that because you were in such a hurry to get to the place you were looking for. You put your hands in the stream, take water with both hands and close your eyes, to wash your face.

(Short pause)

You realize when you open your eyes that you are in another place. That there is no stream or path. You are inside a big bubble and there everything is beautiful. Feel the beating of a heart, perceive the breath, look at a large clock and see a beautiful clarity. You also see a tunnel and at the end, there is a great light. You walk there and when you arrive you see that there is a large mirror that reflects your image in it. At that moment it begins to rain and the rain soaks everything. You keep looking at the mirror and in the image, you are not soaked, you are just there, looking and quietly observing.

(Short pause)

Sitting in front of the mirror, you watch a sunset, a sunset, and a sunrise in front of you. All this happens in very short times, you can hardly understand what you are living. You only understand that your excursion is taking place within yourself. What you were looking for: your inner strength lives in you and you never stopped to feel it or live it consciously.

(Short pause)

You understand that breathing, your heartbeat, time, and inner strength are intimately linked. You become aware of the great responsibility you have for yourself. You recognize the importance of breathing, relaxation, rest, taking care of what you think, what you feel, and what you say. As you reflect, you observe that the rain begins to subside and that a beautiful sun illuminates the place where you are. May the energies of love, health, and well-being accompany you?

(Short pause)

Understand that your inner strength depends on you. You feel that she is there within you, and is always pending and active to support you and to lift you in difficult moments. You understand that this force if not used is atrophied, when we forget ourselves, in our walk through life. You decide after this reflection that you will dedicate more time from now on what you will value every moment of your life as if it were the last. That you will feel worthy of all the good things that the Universe has for you. That you fill your thoughts and emotions with positive energies to always be vibrating in a harmony of peace, harmony, and well-being.

(Short pause)

At that moment, you realize that you are very sleepy, you close your eyes and when you open them you are in your bed, wrapped in your favorite blanket and with your head lying on a very soft pillow. You thank the Universe for the experience and little by little your body falls asleep pleasantly. Good night.

The Great Rock, My Great Purpose

Welcome friend. How nice it is to know that you have taken part of your time to dedicate it to you. You are worthy of that effort that you are making and of all those actions that you can do to achieve your well-being. I inform you that this activity where you are participating, fundamentally seeks that you achieve a pleasant sleep, calm, and relaxation. I wish you success.

(Short pause)

I invite you to find a quiet place in your home, where you do not have interference, where you can carry out this activity with the required privacy. Lie on your bed, with your back straight, your head resting on a soft pillow, but one that keeps your neck relaxed. It is important to stretch your body and be free of any kind of tension or worry,

(Short pause)

What you are going to experience in this experience is intended for you to be able to relax, rest and sleep soundly. This achievement will help you think of new ways to lead your life from now on. It will allow you to draw up new alternatives so that every day you feel happy and renewed. Besides, it will give you tools to initiate healing processes, both of the body and the soul. Therefore, it is important to concentrate and be attentive to the guidance.

(Short pause)

Close your eyes, take a deep breath. You inhale, filling your lungs with renewing energy, and then slowly, you exhale everything that should no longer be in your body. You enjoy and thank the Universe that you can breathe. Check your thoughts and your emotions. If you feel that something disturbs you, give them to the Universe, allow new energies to flow in you and your being to feel free, ready to receive all the good you deserve. Feel the new energies that run through your body to bring you peace, tranquility, and stillness.

(Short pause)

I would like to lovingly remind you that you are a unique being, your experiences and what you have learned from them have determined who you are today. You are capable of achieving everything you set your mind to, valuing every step you advance, and understanding that life is not only about achievements, but also efforts, perseverance, and gratitude. You have to be aware that:

You are an entrepreneurial and resilient being.

You can enjoy every experience that you have to live with an attitude of optimism.

You are a special being with a desire to learn and strengthen yourself every day.

You take life that way because you love yourself.

(Long pause)

At this time, get ready to start a journey with me from your imagination. If at this time you do not want to continue because you are sleepy, there is no problem you can rest, another day you continue. Do not forget that this is the end of this experience.

(Short pause)

Little by little you feel that you are heading towards a special place. You perceive how your body travels through a lighted tunnel, when you leave this you find a beautiful forest. The smell of pine awakens in you the enthusiasm of being there. You begin to walk through that immensity, and you hear a scream in the distance and the song of the birds. You feel a soft but refreshing breeze. You look at the horizon and enjoy the beautiful landscape, where you can see huge mountains and in the distance, you see a large and imposing stone. You experience within your being the desire to run towards it since you cannot see any more path from where you are. You know that you have a long way to go to reach the beautiful and immense rock, but even so, you start your walk towards it.
(Short pause)

You decide to enjoy the road. You appreciate the wildflowers and some animals running around. You are about to enter an area full of beautiful pine trees. You pick up some pine nuts there and put them in a bag that you carry. You enter and observe that in all the pines there are nests, many birds have their home there. That is why the sound of birdsong is louder as you enter that place. You hear how the waters of a stream sound harmoniously on your journey. You are curious to know where the water comes from. You follow the path of the waterfall and notice that there is a water source, which has formed a large well. It is crystalline and sweet water and comes from a mountain.

(Short pause)

You decide to bathe there because the place gives you security and a lot of tranquility. Little by little you wet your feet, then your knees and so each part of your body begins to soak. You realize that the water temperature is perfect, it is neither hot nor cold, and it is warm and you like that. You enjoy submerging your head and your whole body in that place. You move your body, you dance with the harmony of the sounds of the place, feel a lot of happiness inside you. You see that this well is surrounded by white lilies and other yellow flowers that give the place incredible magic. After a while, you leave and start your journey again. (Short pause)

Every step you take, they take you little by little to the beautiful rock that looks out over the horizon. When you arrive at the place, you realize that this rock is very special, because its size is immense and when you approach the cliff, you appreciate that you can advance there. What is coming is avoid. That place serves as a Parador, from that place you can see, on the one hand, large fields and some nearby towns, and on the other, you can look at the sea in the distance. You see imposing mountains, falls, and a waterfall.

(Short pause)

You reflect on your trip and you realize that both the route and the end of the road were beautiful experiences. The road taught you to savor the progress you were making, each stop showed you something, and if you hadn't stopped, it was like your trip would lose meaning. Sometimes we make resolutions, we think only about that goal and it becomes an obsession. However, becoming aware that the path to that goal can also be enjoyed and learning from it is the greatest teaching to live well, better and happier.
(Short pause)

After this reflection, you are grateful for being there, breathing, living, and feeling that great happiness. You sit down to contemplate the landscape and after a while, you lie down near the stone. Little by little your body feels the need to rest. Your eyes close, your entire body relaxes, and you indulge in deep, comforting sleep.

The Butterfly, the Child, and the Context

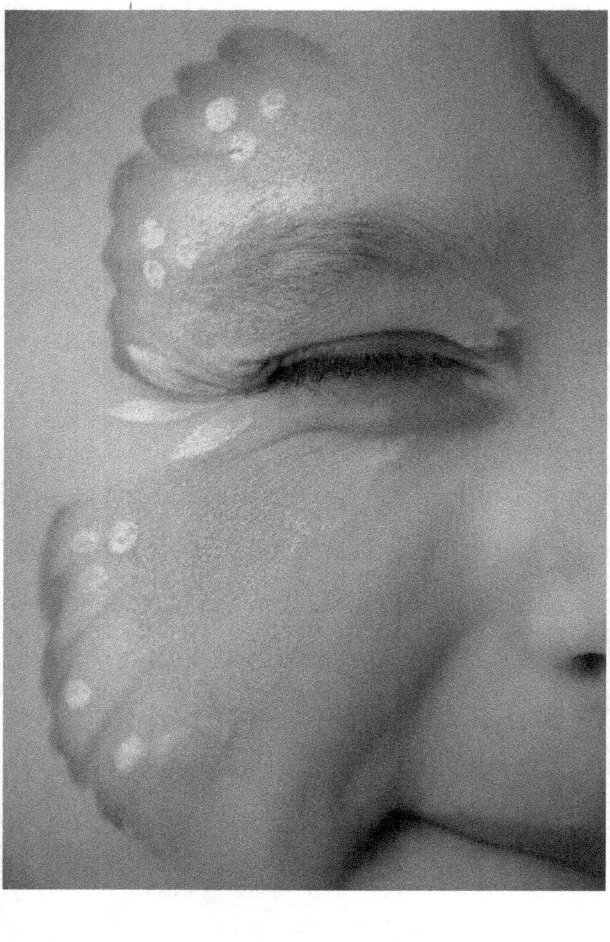

Welcome friend. I sincerely wish you success in this experience that you have decided to live. The main purpose of this activity is to achieve, through guided meditation, that you achieve pleasant sleep, be calm, and relaxed. I invite you to trust in the power of relaxation and the encounter with your internal forces, to achieve healing, peace, harmony, and well-being. (Short pause)

At these times, you must locate yourself in a quiet place, where you have privacy. Lie down on your bed, with your body relaxed, your back straight. Stretch your body, relax your neck, and feel that you are free of tension. Have your favorite pillow on hand, where you will rest your head. Feel that you have lovingly prepared that space to be comfortable, pleased and in this way, you will enjoy this adventure more intensely. (Short pause)

Close your eyes, breathe consciously, inhaling and exhaling. Feel how new energies enter your body that bring you healing and new vibes. Also, when you exhale you perceive that your body becomes light. They do this exercise several times and with each exhalation, you will free yourself from worries and thoughts that distract you, your body is ready to receive and fill with all the good that the Universe has in store for you. You intensely hope to enjoy and be happy.
(Short pause)

You feel that this moment you are living is an opportunity that you have given yourself, to heal both your body and your spirit. You understand that it is important to always make time for yourself, take a break from your usual activities and seek relaxation, calm, and stillness so that your being feels loved and loved by you. You are grateful for being there, and for all that you are experiencing. You internally acknowledge that:

You are capable of promoting transformations in your life that allow you to be happier every day, to be relaxed and calm.

You drive from your inner forces to feel full, loved, and well-being.

(Long pause)

At this time, you must get ready to delve into your imagination and embark on a great adventure. If at this moment, you perceive that you are sleepy and you do not want to continue because your eyes are closed from fatigue, there is no problem you can rest. Remember that this is the main purpose of this experience.

(Short pause)

You decide to embark on your great adventure, so your mind and body move to a large painting workshop. When you look at yourself in a large mirror that is in that room, you see that you are wearing a painter's gown and that you have a color palette in one of your hands and some brushes of various sizes in the other. You realize that you are alone in the place. You notice that there are several blank canvases placed for you to use.

(Short pause)

You breathe deeply. You walk slowly around the place and go through all the spaces. There you see, very beautiful works of art. You see that next to each canvas you have some suggestions of what you should paint. It strikes you that in the suggestions, they do not ask you for anything specific but rather that you paint what comes from your heart. You see that inside the place there is a music player and when you turn it on, a very soft instrumental melody floods the place that pleases you and gives you confidence.

(Short pause)

Then you start to review the suggestions to carry out your works. In one of them, you get a caterpillar covered with fine white threads, between leaves. In another, he looks at a portrait of a little boy and in the other, a white page. They also tell you that you should paint only from your heart. You start to think about each of the suggestions and you feel that they do not make you born anything internally, in those moments. However, you feel like you want to experiment with painting. For this reason, on the first canvas, you start to make very thin strokes of various colors. You take care of the color scheme for this. While doing this exercise, you decide to paint a rainbow. You imagine where the two sides fall and you blur the colors until you achieve a rainbow on top of the lines already made. You also incorporate mountains, rivers, savannah, beaches, houses, and people.

(Short pause)

You feel that this painting represents what is outside of you and that links you with others. When you walk away and see the work, you perceive that you do not appear there represented, but many of the things, people, and elements with which you are identical.

(Short pause)

Then you look at the little caterpillar and decide to paint it. However, you cannot see it because it is covered and hidden. You decide to imagine it, and from your heart, you assign it other colors that it does not have in the sample and you also put wings on it, you begin to discover from within that what you are painting is a beautiful butterfly. For this reason, you incorporate into the caterpillar some elements that transform its image and turn it into a work full of creativity. You realize that the butterfly is certainly one of the most interesting species and that its metamorphosis process is transforming its essence until it becomes works of art. You become aware of the importance of looking at others not only for what they appear but also for their essence of being. You value at that moment the capacity for transformation of human beings and other species.

(Short pause)

Then you go to where the portrait of the child is. At that moment, you remember your childhood, the beautiful moments of that stage, the love you received, and also think about what you have become. Instead of brushes you take some charcoals and start the last paintwork. You start at the bottom to paint a child that represents all the feelings you remember from that age, then you paint the face of a young man accompanied by symbols of the activities that you liked the most, then you paint your inner adult. In the end, you place some fine lines that indicate the transcendence of being. This work was abstract, where there was a great connection between childhood, living as a young man, and maturity.

(Short pause)

After this great adventure, you sit down to contemplate what has been done and you perceive that your inner being is satisfied. This adventure lived I invite you to become aware of what surrounds you, to look at those who share with you in their essence and their capacity for transformation. Also, to understand that life is a great journey and that the child that lived in you is still there. And although you evolved and matured, what you received as a child is what you are today. Little by little you feel a deep sleep, you are tired and you want to rest. Your eyes close on their own, you yearn to be in your warm bed and sleep soundly. Good night.

A Garden of Dreams

Welcome, mate, to our meditation session. Today we are going to join in a wonderful journey that will take you into a new space for you, a place that will allow you to rediscover the calm you need, relax and live such a pleasant experience that will lead you to fall into a revitalizing sleep for that you achieve the peace that you long for.

(Short pause)

To begin with our meeting, I want to invite you to find a serene place that makes you feel free and calm, where you can sit in a comfortable chair or lie down on your soft bed and fully stretch your body, keeping your back straight, relaxing your neck and thus releasing all the tensions that may be within you at this moment.

(Long pause)

Now that you are physically prepared, it is time to prepare your head so close your eyes little by little so that you can concentrate solely on emptying your mind of any thoughts that may be a cause for discomfort and concern. Let go of all the problems that afflict you and you will be able to be open to the emotions and sensations that you will soon experience and that will make you feel like someone completely renewed.

(Middle pause)

At this point, we are almost ready to start your journey, so I want to remind you why you are here: this is your moment, one that you are allowing yourself to live to fill you with relaxation and peace. We are together so that you can feel full, that you can see what life has to offer you, and delight yourself with all the beauty that Mother Nature can create only for you.

(Middle pause)

The Universe has extraordinary things to give you
because you are a profoundly wonderful being.
You are someone special and covered in love.
You are made to bring harmony to those around you.

You are a being full of a lot of light and an enormous brightness.

You are full of good vibes and great value to face any situation you have to face.

You are a perfect creation of the Universe.

(Long pause)

You start to feel as if your mind is taking you more and more within it and it is time to immerse yourself in the stillness that you experience and to allow yourself to be one with the Universe. Before you complete your trip, I want to tell you that there is no problem if you want to sleep before finishing our meeting, that is what we are looking for and you can always continue later. Now you feel like you are back in control of your body and experience a sweet scent.

(Middle pause)

You allow yourself to enjoy the sweet aroma that floods your body making your senses fly and that way you can notice that it seems to be that of a million fresh flowers, then you decide to open your eyes to see where you are and the thought that you could not be in a better place comes to your mind: you are standing in the middle of a huge and fascinating garden full of grass, trees, and flowers so brightly colored that they make you feel full of life and vigor.

(Short pause)

Everything as far as your eye can see seems to be magical and comes from one of your best dreams, that's why you don't wait any longer and start walking through the grass that with its softness makes you feel as if you are floating on the clouds with every little step you take, and it is that beautiful sensation that makes you take off your shoes to enjoy it much more and connect with nature. In doing so, the brush between the grass and your feet is something completely new for you and fills your body with emotion as you feel as free as never before.

(Middle pause)

The freedom you experience is something that at another time would have seemed unimaginable and leads you to run through the fabulous landscape in which you find yourself. While you accelerate your speed, you feel that the pure air caresses your face and that the leaves of the trees surround you, hugging you warmly, all in such a special way that it gives you the impression that you are flying around the garden so you decide to take advantage of something so extraordinary and you close your eyes to let yourself be guided to where the wind wants to take you.

(Long pause)

After minutes of rejoicing with the magnificent sensation that the Universe gave you, you feel how slowly your body is deposited back on the ground so you open your eyes to re-enchant yourself with the grace of the place and when you observe what surrounds you right now, a big smile happens to be drawn on your face. The space that is right in front of you is decorated with beautiful flowers of millions of quite varied colors, of different types that go from the largest to the smallest and that have such an exquisite smell that it makes you feel intoxicated with the feeling so deep of peace and happiness within you.

(Middle pause)

Then you get closer and the closer you do, the aroma of honey and cinnamon intensifies so much that it fills your lungs allowing your soul to enter a state of abysmal serenity. Suddenly, you have a strong desire to lay down your body to fill yourself with tranquility, recharge your batteries and continue enjoying the wonders that life presents to you. So when searching the ground, you get a small place in the middle of the flowers and their buds, so that you can lie down and look up at the sky.

(Short pause)

By resting your body on the grass, you begin to see up to the horizon and contemplate the flight of hundreds of birds that seem to parade before you, letting you be dazzled by the elegance of their movements. Later you fix your attention on the sweet flow of the clouds that combines perfectly with the beautiful blue of the majestic sky, and it is there when you realize that the dream has taken over you. Your mind begins to empty to give rise to the sensation that you lose control of your extremities while your eyes begin to feel tired and to close very slowly, raising your consciousness on a journey as delicate as that of the birds you previously observed.

(Short pause)

Sweet dreams, dear partner.

The Island of Enchantment

Welcome, friend, this is our meditation session: a space in your life that you will dedicate to seeking the relaxation you need for your rest. Together we will embark on a journey with which you will be able to experience beautiful sensations that will make you feel serene. Today we will make you achieve a pleasant dream that will allow you to fill you with energy to continue peacefully with your day-to-day.

(Short pause)

At this time I want to ask you to go to a place where you can sit in a chair, settle on your bed, or any place that allows you to be calm. The most important thing is that you are comfortable and that you manage to fully stretch your body, keeping your back straight and relaxing your neck. All of this will help you stay calm and release all your physical tensions.

(Long pause)

Now that you are ready, you will need to close your eyes to get to the bottom of your mind and free it of all its thoughts. At this moment it is time to free yourself from all your chains: you must get rid of any ideas about the external world that may be within you, let go of what may distract you to focus only on yourself and on the extraordinary experience that you will soon be able to experience.

(Short pause)

I want to let you know that this will be a unique moment, something completely magical that will be full of relaxation and peace, what you need to heal your spirit and find your north. Starting today you will get a fascinating experience in which you will delight in the beauty of what the Universe has created only to make you feel serene and to show you everything you deserve to be whom you are.

(Short pause)

You are a being of light.

You are life and purity.

Your soul is filled with the courage you need to live that life you dream of.

You are full of good energies that will make you completely successful with everything you want to achieve.

You are a being of peace.

Your body is full of love and wonderful vibes that perfectly complement your beautiful spirit.

You are beautiful and unique.

(Long pause)

Listening to what fills you with fantastic emotions that make you immerse yourself inside yourself to see what the Universe has prepared for you today. Before you start your trip, I want you to know that there is no problem if you feel that the dream takes over you before finishing our experience because that is what we want, so calm down. You begin to go much deeper into your mind and feel fulfilled, then you understand: the journey has begun.

(Middle pause)

You enter a kind of portal inside your mind that takes you directly to your expected place. At this moment you feel that a strong wind touches your face and passes through your entire body, letting you breathe in a pure and fresh air that enters your lungs filling them with great vitality.

(Short pause)

The natural breeze of the place where you are makes you want to open your eyes and when you follow your instinct you see that you are standing on what seems to be a beautiful island, then you decide to observe everything in detail and the mere fact of seeing the small grains of the clear sand in which your feet melt as if they already felt a part of it makes you enchanted. Also, the contact of your body with the warmth of the ground allows you to enjoy the feeling of rejoicing in its cozy welcome that feels like a warm hug.

(Middle pause)

The soft sound of the waves breaking against the sand makes you occupy your attention in them. The water that surrounds the place where you turn out to be the most crystalline you have seen and not satisfied with that, it is also calm and calm so it produces a nice feeling of happiness and you decide to take a little of it in your hands to wet your hair slowly and fill yourself with that wonderful liquid created by the Universe for you. As you feel fresh, you begin to perceive that peace floods you and that life could not be more incredible with you than it is now, so you inhale deeply to fill your being with everything that you currently experience.

(Short pause)

With your hair dripping little by little on you and making you laugh with the sensation of the drops brushing your back, you think about sitting on the sand to refresh yourself a little more with that fantastic substance that makes you think that you are living a dream. The hypnotic swaying of the waves makes your legs fill with its water slowly and the serenity that causes you to feel connected with Mother Nature is something magical so you start looking up to the sky to enjoy the sun that offers you a wonderful sight to be hidden behind a great mountain and that at the same time shelters you with its strong rays, making you feel protected and giving you the energy you need.

(Middle pause)

A smile comes to your face when you can watch in the distance how beautiful dolphins go in and out of the water as if they were performing a sensational act just for you with which they allow you to admire their fabulous skills and listen to them making their funny sounds. Even when you thought that nothing could overcome something like this, the legendary experience is completed when a group of birds with beautiful colors begin to fly over you, making you lie down on the sand to stare at their charm and they as if they understood your intentions begin to sing a beautiful melody that leads you to close your eyes to allow you to enjoy his song at the moment in which you thank the Universe for the surprising adventure that I devised for you.

(Long pause)

While you are grateful to have the opportunity to breathe one more day, you begin to experience that fatigue that fills your body and happy to notice that you will soon achieve your goal, you let yourself be carried away by the majestic sound of the birds until the deep sleep that soon embraces you to give you the best rest you've ever had.

(Middle pause)

Good night my friend.

A Visit to Heaven

Hello friend, welcome to our meditation session. This will be a time when we will dedicate ourselves to the search for the calm and relaxation that you long for in your life. Today we will take a trip through your mind to know the wonderful things that the Universe has planned for you and so that you can finally achieve a deep and pleasant sleep that will fill you with energy.

(Short pause)

Now I want to invite you to find a quiet place where you can sit on a chair or lie in the comfort of your bed so that you stretch your body perfectly, keeping your back straight and relaxing your neck. That way, your physical state can calm down and feel at peace so that soon we can focus solely on your mind and spirit.

(Middle pause)

Approaching the beginning of your journey, I must ask you to close your eyes: do it calmly and serenely, now nothing can hurt you because it is only you and me. Concentrate only on you and empty your mind of any thoughts that may distract you from what you will soon experience, let go of each of the problems, the situations that go around your head, and all the conflicts that are in you because now only you matter.

(Middle pause)

I want to remind you that this is a moment of relaxation and peace, in this time that you are allowing yourself to enjoy, you and I will be giving pause to the outside world to focus on you and everything that the Universe gives you: today You will be able to find your north, heal your spirit and enjoy the tranquility that all the new sensations that only you will have the joy of experiencing will generate.

(Short pause)

The Universe loves you and that is why it has wonderful things in store for you.

You are a being of peace.

You are full of light.

You radiate love and shine with every step you take and action you take.

You are a unique creation of the Universe that gave you all the existing qualities so that your life is full of happiness.

You are worthy of all the great things you want to achieve.

(Long pause)

The sound of my voice that reminds you of all the magnificent qualities that are in you, makes you go much deeper into your mind and that causes you to slowly travel the dark space in it: you are immersing yourself in the journey. But before you continue, I want to tell you that it is okay if you want to sleep instead of ending our experience: that is precisely our goal and everything will be fine if it is fulfilled earlier than planned, so keep calm. You begin to feel that you are entering a tunnel in which there is a beautiful light and you decide to get closer and closer to it, when you finally enter it, your soul takes control of you and you feel in a soft and very comfortable space: we have arrived at our destination.

(Middle pause)

You are sitting on some surface so spongy that it makes you feel as if you are in the same sky and surprisingly you confirm it when you open your eyes you can see that you are in what appears to be a large white and delicate cloud that moves through the precious blue. The softness and firmness of the cloud are so impressive that you experience the sensation that your body is placed on a huge cotton ball and it is that thought that makes you want to catch a little of it in your hand. When you start it, you start to play and caress it while you delight in its fabulous texture.

(Middle pause)

Impressed by the magnificent idea of having a piece of heaven in your hands, you begin to feel completely happy with the sensation of perceiving yourself as the owner of the world and the knowledge that the Universe has created that experience only for you, fills your soul with rejoicing and joy because at this moment you feel worthy of anything on the globe, you feel that after this day you have the strength and the certainty of being able to achieve each of your goals and beyond that, you feel immense love for yourself and for the life you are lucky to live.

(Long pause)

As you reflect on the wonders of life, a strong breeze comes to you that moves your hair from one side to the other and that does not make you cold but embraces you warmly, making you inhale with all you might to keep inside you a little of that fantastic air. Upon entering your body, oxygen feels like a gift from heaven that fills you, cleanse your lungs, and purifies your soul, surrounding it with peace and tranquility at the thought that there is no better place you could be.

(Middle pause)

As another surprise of the Universe for you, at the end of the air current, the cloud in which you are sitting begins to move to one side along with others to give way to the majestic Sun that slowly rises giving you the possibility of contemplating it in its maximum splendor, to admire how it illuminates everything in its path and above all, to warm your whole body with its great rays of light and you, welcomed by the warmth that is given to you and enjoying the slow movement of the cloud, you decide to lie on it to still relax plus.

(Short pause)

When you rest your body on the cloud, the thought of how good life is being with you returns to you and how lucky you are to experience things as impressive as the ones you live now. Then you realize that the Universe knew exactly what to give you in this, your moment because it has undoubtedly given you wonderful experiences that have filled your soul and spirit with the peace you longed for.

(Middle pause)

Feeling so full and fortunate with what you have, you begin to perceive that fatigue takes over your body and you understand: the moment for which you have come has arrived, the time of rest that you wanted is about to begin. Understanding this, you close your eyes and adjust your body to quickly fall into a deep and revitalizing sleep.

(Middle pause)

Sweet Dreams friend.

The Jungle of Dreams

You are welcome friend, to our meditation session. This will be a moment that we will both dedicate to you, in the search for your calm and your relaxation, and that is why I am here. I will be your companion on the magnificent journey that you will undertake today, a walk in which you will know a wonderful place that will allow you to achieve a totally pleasant dream.

(Short pause)

To begin our adventure, I want to ask you to find a quiet place away from the noise and everything that can distract you from what you will experience. Find a space where you can sit on a chair or lie on your bed, there you must stretch your body, relax your neck and keep your back straight so that you can release all the tensions that are inside you.

(Middle pause)

Now you must close your eyes and stay calm, concentrate on the silence and what is inside you. Go into the depths of your mind and empty it of any kind of thoughts. Get rid of all the emotional burdens you carry and ditch the bad vibes to allow in all the good that will soon come and that will make you feel like someone new and renewed.

(Middle pause)

Today we are gathered by and for you, this time that you dedicate was a great decision to open the doors of your soul to happiness and good energy. This is a moment of relaxation and peace, it is a pause from daily life in which you can find your north and heal your spirit, connecting with nature and its creations in a fantastic place that you will soon know.

(Short pause)

You are a pure and wonderfully beautiful being.

You emanate light and happiness.

You are full of good vibes and fantastic energies that will soon come out so that you can find the tranquility that you are looking for so much.

Your soul carries a great list of beautiful things.

Your chest protects a huge heart full of beautiful feelings.

You are loaded with kindness and generosity.

You are love, you are peace and you are shine.

(Long pause)

The moments in which you have believed in all the good things that are within you and that have made you immensely happy appear in your head as you go through your mind on the journey to the longed-for site of our meeting. I want to tell you that there is no problem in case you want to fall asleep instead of ending our trip, remember that this is what we are looking for, so you can always continue at another time. The memories slowly disappear to give way to a great door that you open to finally reach the place that the Universe has prepared for you.

(Middle pause)

When you enter the room behind the door, you can see how everything that was dark before turns into a very green space full of trees. Looking at what is around you, you decide to start walking a bit to start your journey through the fabulous site that awaits you. As you walk you can see that space is much larger than you thought and you delight in the beautiful terrain full of grass and some plants that are the largest you have ever seen, so you start to see the whole territory with a lot of attention because it is really special.

(Middle pause)

Something moves in the distance and you calmly wait to see what is coming. Your face lights up with excitement when you see that what moves between the trees is a huge giraffe that walks towards the plants that it easily reaches with its magnificent statue and you take a moment to admire the dazzling elegance that it exudes with each step it takes. The giraffe watches you carefully and you do the same with it and then continue on your way when the animal is dedicated to eating some leaves.

(Short pause)

Your joy increases when you see a charming lioness that walks through the place very slowly, taking firm steps with its robust legs and your surprise is gigantic when you see that behind her some little lions come playing with each other whom you recognize as her children. The mother of the family walks with such confidence that she hypnotizes you and her babies are so entertained playing that they make you laugh a few laughs when you see them bite their tails and ears. The world seems to be paralyzed at the time in which a roar is heard that makes many birds fly demonstrating why lions are known as the kings of the jungle and later a huge lion appears in your field of vision that seems to be responsible for the thunderous roar. Looking at it is extraordinary:

(Middle pause)

The warm sun of the place makes you feel embraced by its fantastic rays and little by little your soul feels more and more happy and relaxed by the peace that this space transmits that welcomes you as if you were part of it from the beginning. Then as you go through everything, you see a fascinating group of zebras that eat the grass of the place and that lets you get close to touching them, showing you that the surprises are not over yet. The texture of their fur is even more incredible than their beautiful stripes and the calm that feels their loins generates is so great that as if something were telling you, you begin to follow them when they begin to walk slowly through their territory. (Short pause)

From one moment to another, the zebras stop and move aside leaving you in the middle of the space, and when you take what seems to be an invitation to walk forward you can see a huge bed covered by the shadow of many trees. Then you understand that it is time to take a break and lie down on the bed that is the softest you have ever been in. Your body slowly relaxes and enjoys the fabulous view that the leaves of the trees and the beautiful sky give you, fatigue manifests itself and your consciousness is lost in the immensity while your eyes close little by little to fall asleep in a deep sleep.

(Middle pause)

Good night, dear friend.

A Delicious Break

Welcome, partner, this is our meditation session: a space prepared for you, for your rest and tranquility. Today I will be your companion on a wonderful journey that aims to achieve calm and relaxation, all for a single objective: to get you to get a pleasant and restful sleep that allows you to fill yourself with energy and good vibes for your life.

(Short pause)

Before we start our journey, I want to ask you to find a quiet place where you can lie on your bed or even sit on a comfortable chair. The important thing is that you manage to be serene and that you stretch your body completely so that you keep your back straight and your neck relaxed, this will help you free yourself from the tensions accumulated in your body so that you are physically prepared for everything that awaits you.

(Middle pause)

Now is the time to close your eyes and empty your mind of all the thoughts that are in it, let go of any overwhelming idea that may be disturbing you, eliminate problems, and break the chains that prevent you from moving towards peace and tranquility because When you achieve that, you will be able to reach a state that will allow you to open up for all the sensations that you will experience and the good vibes that you will receive from this incredible journey.

(Middle pause)

I want you to know that taking this time for yourself was an excellent decision. This is a pause in which you can forget about the outside world, focus on yourself, and seek your north and the healing of your spirit. The journey that awaits you will take you on a wonderful path that will make you discover fantastic things and experience new sensations with which you will learn to enjoy life.

(Short pause)

You are an extraordinary and special being.

You have a valuable and courageous soul.

You are a magnificent person and charged with a great inner light.

Your heart is full of love.

You are in this world for a reason: you are someone who will fill those around him with his light and infect the world with his joy.

You are valuable and capable of achieving everything you dream of.

(Long pause)

Thinking of everything you dream of fills your mind with all the peace that allows you to start with the expected journey. I want you to know that if the dream comes to you before ending our experience, you can leave in peace, that is what we want for you and you can come back another day to finish our trip. The memories are lost until you see a beautiful light that calls you to come closer, when you are about to enter you close your eyes and you begin to feel a gentle tingling throughout your body: you have reached your destination.

(Middle pause)

Feeling that the sunlight warms your body in a cozy way, you decide to open your eyes to find out where the Universe has taken you and when you do, you find yourself inside a huge landscape full of green grass that you can appreciate, it spreads as far as the eye can see but with precious details of vivid colors given by beautiful flowers that you can locate in some areas. The bright touches of the color of the plants manage to highlight the beauty of the place much more and that is why you decide that you should not miss the opportunity to get closer to them to delight your eyes much more.

(Short pause)

When you reach the first flower zone, you can feel the delicious smell of cinnamon that makes your senses fly and allows you to enjoy much more of the fabulous experience that only the magic of nature could recreate. Then, as another sample of the wonders that the Universe has destined for you, some bees approach, going from flower to flower, spreading color wherever they go, as in a synchronized dance to extract their pollen. The contrast of the vibrant yellow color with the solid black that as a work of art dresses the cute animals, surprises and hypnotizes you to the point where when they have finished their work and leave, you follow them to see where they are going.

(Short pause)

Only a few minutes pass in which you walk around the meadow accompanying your new friends who stop when they reach a beautiful tree with a robust trunk and branches full of beautiful leaves decorated with a beautiful red color. When you get much closer to the majestic place, you see that the bees enter a large honeycomb that looks completely perfect when you have them going from one place to another, working to make their attractive honey that overflows from the honeycomb emanating an exquisite aroma that causes you to wet your Finger on it to taste its flavor that makes your heart jump with happiness because you have never tasted something as wonderful and pure as that gift of nature.

(Middle pause)

You get a great surprise when you feel a strong breeze that runs through your body as in a gentle hug and that also causes some leaves to fall to the ground forming a large cluster of them on which you decide to lie down to enjoy the shade that the tree and continue savoring a little more of the sweet taste of honey. As you lie down on the leaves, you feel that your body rests on soft cotton, as if nature had given you a soft bed in which you could rest to assimilate all the surprises it has given you.

(Short pause)

When you remember everything you have lived, your chest swells with happiness thinking about how lucky you are to have had such wonderful experiences, and you begin to be grateful for having the joy of being alive while looking up at the beautiful blue sky. Slowly, your body begins to feel tired and the idea comes to you that the desired moment has arrived: it is time to rest quietly. You close your eyes and perceive that your limbs feel light, almost as if you had become one of the leaves on which you find yourself, to fly up to the sky and lose yourself in the clouds, surrendering to the deep sleep that now welcomes you.

(Middle pause)

Sweet dreams, mate.

The Streets of Calm

Welcome, dear companion, to our meditation session: a small space prepared exclusively for you, for the search and the reach of calm and relaxation that you need so much in your life and that will lead you to a pleasant and revitalizing sleep that will fill you of the necessary energies to continue with your life happily and fully.

(Short pause)

At this time I want to invite you to go to a quiet space where you can sit on a comfortable chair or simply lie down on your soft bed to obtain the calm you require. You must relax your neck, keep your back straight, and stretch your body so that it releases all its physical tensions and is prepared for the sensations that you will experience.

(Middle pause)

Now that your body is relaxed, you will need to get your mind ready because it must be empty to receive all the good things that will come to you very soon. You will do this by closing your eyes and concentrating on the silence that surrounds you, disconnect from the world, and enter your mind by opening its doors and windows to strip it of all bad thoughts, unsolved problems, your internal conflicts, and situations that may overwhelm you.

(Short pause)

This moment is meant for you, it was made so that you could give a break to everything else and focus solely on yourself, on the peace that you will receive and the relaxation that will take hold of you when you start your way through the streets of calm and you can see the beautiful colors of the world that the Universe has recreated so that you can admire all the good it has to offer you.

(Middle pause)

You are the bearer of magical things that are made to come to light.

You are love.

You are peace.

You are loaded with life.

You are light and pure.

The Universe has created a wonderful plan for you and your life will be full of tranquility, happiness, and successes that will make you be someone wholesome.

You are full of positive vibes and energies.

You are a being that radiates charm and charisma.

(Long pause)

As you listen to my voice, your spirit begins its journey around your mind, letting you see beautiful moments in which you have been someone really happy. Before you reach your destination, I want to tell you that there will be no problem if you want to go to sleep instead of ending our experience because we are here to seek that you can sleep peacefully, and if that happens, we will have achieved our goal, so calm down, friend. The memories are becoming more and more distant and instead, you see a great tunnel through which you start walking to find a door that you decide to enter: we have finished the trip.

(Short pause)

When you open your eyes you can see a fantastic landscape before you: you are standing right in the middle of a huge road, which is surrounded on one side by large buildings and the other, by a beautiful beach that gives the place a unique freshness. Only the thought of how beautiful the view is from where you are is located in your head: the sky seems to have been drawn by the best painter of all that have been able to exist, being a combination of beautiful orange and purple colors that together you They give the feeling of being in paradise itself, so you decide to stay watching to save every possible detail of that beautiful panorama.

(Middle pause)

When you feel that you have finished detailing as much as possible of the majestic sky, you walk a little to place your gaze on the beautiful buildings that adorn the space with their large size: their exquisite pastel colors give more life to the place and their glass windows reflect the glimpses of the sun and the magnificent beach right in front of them. Then you take other steps to focus on the water, which is so crystalline that like the buildings, it creates a fabulous reflection of the fascinating landscape, making it even more precious with each sweet movement of the tide that is as calm as everything else.

(Short pause)

Then you begin to wonder how it is that being such an impressive city there does not seem to be anyone around that like you, enjoys the view. At that moment the answer comes to your mind as if the solution to your question had always been within you, it is simple: the Universe has created all that beauty only for you because that place is just as charming as your soul, because it keeps in the all the beauty of your heart and because your spirit is an accumulation of beautiful qualities and that makes you worthy of all that and much more.

(Long pause)

Seeing that these affirmations come from the bottom of your soul, the joy that is deposited in your heart is enormous and your chest swells with pride and happiness when you finally understand everything incredible that is inside you and that your spirit is capable to create things as fascinating as where you stand. Those feelings fill you with a peace that you have never felt, something that is bigger than all the buildings in the place, stronger than the rays of the sun, and purer than the water on the beach, today you understand that you are capable of achieving all your dreams; your life is a gift to the world, and you that with each breath you bring light and shine to the Universe that loves you as the best of its beings.

(Middle pause)

As you smile skyward to thank you for all the gifts you have had the joy of receiving today, a strong but welcoming breeze slowly lifts you into the air and gives you a new perspective of space that looks even more impressive from above. When floating, you realize how tired you are and little by little you feel that your body no longer belongs to you when your eyes are slowly closing. Suddenly you feel that you are deposited in the softest bed you have ever tried and, letting yourself be carried away by your desires, you fall into the deepest and most pleasant sleep you have ever had.

(Middle pause)

Sweet dreams, dear partner.

A Walk along the Beach

Welcome, my friend, today we will have a beautiful meditation session in which with my help, you will have the joy of achieving the calm and relaxation that you want for your life, all through a trip that will make you enjoy the wonders of the world, and be grateful to breathe one more day. It will be that joy, the one that will lead you to achieve a pleasant dream that will provide you with the energy you need.

(Short pause)

I want to invite you to look for space where you can be calm and comfortable, something away from the outside world, a place where you can focus only on yourself and where you can sit in a nice chair or the comfort of your bed so that you stretch your body, keep your back straight, relax your neck and thus release all your physical tensions.

(Middle pause)

Now you must close your eyes slowly and immerse yourself confidently inside your mind, do it little by little, analyzing everything that is in it and letting it go: erase each of the bad thoughts within you, drive away from the sadness, undo the regrets and keep that prodigious space free for the good vibes and positive energies to enter to establish peace and tranquility within you.

(Middle pause)

The moment you are living is something magical and fascinating that will take you to experience new and incredible sensations. Very soon you will be able to start living things that will help you find your north and heal your spirit in a splendid journey that you will take accompanied by a fantastic friend whom you will soon meet and who will help you fill with deep peace and relaxation.

(Middle pause)

You are someone full of good things and beautiful feelings.

You have great potential to succeed in everything you set your mind to.

You deserve the best the Universe has to offer you.

You are a persistent and capable being.

You have everything you need to shine and fulfill your dreams.

You are about to live a wonderful stage that will give you everything you need to be deeply happy.

(Long pause)

The powerful affirmations that you hear make you feel complete and fulfilled, you experience for the first time the feeling that you are someone complete and that you can achieve everything that you propose, then totally relaxed, you begin to lose yourself between the paths of your mind. I want you to know that if you feel that you need to sleep before ending our experience, you can do it quietly because that is what we are looking for today. You begin to feel that your spirit takes control of your body and you let yourself be guided by it through a great tunnel that will take you to the longed-for meeting.

(Middle pause)

When you open your eyes you get the beautiful view of a great beach with beautiful water as blue as the sky under which it is, which is full of wonderfully white clouds that look like huge cotton balls rigorously placed to decorate harmoniously space. The landscape in front of you brings to mind the idea that it looks as if it had been the best painting by the most experienced artist, and you are right: the author of this work is the Universe that has given you his most beautiful work so you can see how much he loves you and how important you are to him.

(Middle pause)

Your soul is infected with the tranquility of the tide in front of which you are standing and your heart beats slowly while you remain ecstatic by what you can see and by the melodious sound of the small waves crashing against a beautiful lighthouse located right on the shore.

(Long pause)

From one moment to the next, your attention is absorbed by a wonderful white horse like the clouds in the sky, galloping towards you with the elegance that only an animal as impressive and robust as that could have. Its main and tail move from side to side with the rapidity of its steps that generate a completely relaxing sound. In a short time, the beautiful being is in front of you, lowering its head showing you that it is there to serve you and you give free rein to your desire to caress its soft fur that provides you with a deep peace as soon as you can touch it.

(Middle pause)

After a while in which you caress it and enjoy the tranquility that it gives you, the hair bends down making you see that it wants you to mount it and you, placing all your trust in it, decide to get on its back so that later the animal stands up. Stand up and start walking slowly, allowing you to admire the beauty of the place from a new perspective and enjoy the extraordinary walk you are taking.

(Short pause)

As they walk along the beach, the sun begins to set, starting a majestic sunset with the most beautiful combination of pink and orange tones that colors the sky, making what before seemed perfect now be overcome before your very eyes. Those rays of sun that still refuse to go are reflected in the water creating fabulous flashes of light that further adorn the panorama and for its part, the slow and hypnotic movement of the tide, combined with the beautiful bubbles formed by the animals that They make their living in the water put the finishing touches on the artwork that you feel deeply fortunate to witness.

(Middle pause)

The horse that has become your guide through the magnificent adventure, begins to slow down its steps to later lie down right next to a pillow that is on the shore of the beach. Something inside you knows that it is time to rest and that your partner has taken you to that place because that pillow is the last gift for you, so you decide to lie next to him in the sand and put your head on the pillow that is one of the softest you've ever used. You start again to caress your friend to enjoy the contact between his body and your hands again. Little by little your body begins to relax completely, making you dedicate yourself solely to seeing the sky until you begin to feel so tired that your eyes slowly close, finally letting you enter a pleasant sleep.

(Middle pause)

Good night my friend.

Rest in the Snow

Welcome, friend, to our meditation today. You and I will travel together in this time that will be destined for you to achieve calm and total relaxation so that you achieve a pleasant and deep sleep that will allow you to recharge all your energies and continue like this, traveling the beautiful paths of life.

(Short pause)

So that we start with our charming meeting, I advise you to look for a quiet place where you can feel free, relax your spirit and seek the calm you need. For this to happen, I recommend you sit on a chair or lie down in the comfort of your bed so that you stretch your body, relax your neck, keep your back straight and release all your tensions.

(Middle pause)

Now close your eyes slowly, friend, you must concentrate on what you will live in this moment, on what is inside you, and on emptying your mind. Forget everything that can disturb your mind and tense your body because this moment is only yours and the only thing that matters is the tranquility you want. So push away all the bad energies so you can give way to the good vibes.

(Middle pause)

We all need a moment of relaxation to pause and forget about the outside world, that's why you are here: this will be a moment of peace and tranquility where we seek to find your north and heal your spirit. Today you will be able to enjoy a beautiful trip in which you will meet an impressive site and great companions who will teach you beautiful things and help you see life in a better way.

(Short pause)

You are the owner of your world.

You live a beautiful life that makes you happy.

You are a valuable and persevering being.

The Universe loves you and values your existence in it.

You are someone happy and positive.

You are full of love.

You are a wise, strong, and successful being.

You have a free and prosperous spirit.

You are lucky and you are full of good vibes and positive energies.

(Long pause)

Your body slowly begins to relax, you feel your limbs relax, and your spirit begins to fly through your mind: you are beginning our journey. Before you continue your journey, I want to clarify that if at any time you feel that you need to rest, there will be no problem because what we are looking for is that you can have a peaceful sleep and you can always have another opportunity to return to end our meeting. Now you feel a soft cold near you and this is how you feel that you have reached your destination.

(Middle pause)

The cold you feel in your body rather than making you feel uncomfortable, generates the feeling that you are in your element and when you open your eyes to see where this temperature comes from, you see that all you can look around is a completely white space: there are hundreds of huge trees covered in thick and beautiful snow that decorates the entire site with its fantastic color, plus there are large amounts of water turned into beautiful ice. But the most important thing is that far beyond the cold air that expands through the place, peace is the factor that reigns and is breathed in the environment that is alone, giving you a fascinating feeling of freedom that makes you draw a big smile on your face.

(Short pause)

When you start to walk forward, you discover that a group of beautiful dogs with beautiful and abundant fur is approaching you pulling a large sled. The animals' beauty surprises you but your surprise increases when they stop right in front of you and you start stroking them to please your desire to feel their hair. The moment your hands touch the body of the dogs, your soul is filled with joy and joy with the connection you perceive and the positive energy that they transmit to you with a simple contact, so you allow yourself to enjoy that incredible feeling.

(Middle pause)

After a few minutes in which you only dedicate yourself to caressing the fur of the animals, they begin to bark at you but they don't scare you: you understand that they want to tell you something even though you don't know how to know exactly what. Therefore, while you see them without understanding what they hope to get from you, you realize that their eyes speak louder than words: they are asking you to get into the vehicle to take a ride with you, then you listen to them and sit inside the transport to tell them that they can start their journey. The moment you finish pronouncing your words, they begin to walk gently through the snow, making you relax extraordinarily by observing the entire landscape and showing you that your authorization was the only thing they were waiting for to advance.

(Short pause)

As you walk through the snow, some flakes fall on you in what seems to be the beginning of a snowy rain that makes you laugh at the thought that you become part of space by having small pieces of white ice on you.

(Short pause)

When your gaze returns to the panorama you can see everything in detail: some arctic foxes observe you calmly and then continue running around the place, you also see a huge polar bear walking very serene and confident knowing that on the top of a mountain that is its space, and finally you have the fantastic pleasure of finding a small ice-water well in which the dogs stop so that you can contemplate how large and small fish of different colors swim through it, going from one place to another.

(Short pause)

After spending a few minutes appreciating the dogs that took you around the site, you begin to realize how lucky you are: the Universe has created this experience for you because you are a wonderful person and you are here to see that just breathing is a gift and that living another day is a new opportunity to be happy.

(Middle pause)

So while you thank the Universe for everything you have lived, you begin to let yourself flow between the breeze, the snowflakes that still fall on your face, and the serenity that is inside your heart. Little by little you settle into the sled and feel your consciousness fade as your eyes begin to slowly close to giving way to resting in a deep and pleasant sleep.

(Middle pause)

Sweet Dreams friend.